A Gift Like Zoe's

C. C. Holmes

C. C. Holmes/A Gift Like Zoe's
Printed in the United States of America

This is a work of fiction. Names, characters, places, and incidents are a product of the author's imagination. Locales and public names are sometimes used for atmospheric purposes. Any resemblance to actual people, living or dead, or to businesses, companies, events, institutions, or locales is completely coincidental.

A Gift Like Zoe's/C. C. Holmes -- 1st ed.

ISBN 978-0-9963966-7-7 Print Edition
ISBN 978-0-9963966-8-4 Ebook Edition

To Chris,
for being the magic spark
that lights my path
on this spiritual journey
of ours.

O, believe, as thou livest, that every sound that is spoken over the round world, which thou oughtest to hear, will vibrate on thine ear! Every proverb, every book, every byword that belongs to thee for aid or comfort, shall surely come home through open or winding passages. Every friend whom not thy fantastic will, but the great and tender heart in thee craveth, shall lock thee in his embrace. And this, because the heart in thee is the heart of all; not a valve, not a wall, not an intersection is there anywhere in nature, but one blood rolls uninterruptedly an endless circulation through all men, as the water of the globe is all one sea, and, truly seen, its tide is one.

Ralph Waldo Emerson
Essays: First Series
"The Over-Soul"

Chapter One

Zoe couldn't wait to get to the deli to grab lunch. A good sandwich and energy drink would ease her hangover from last night's school-is-out-for-the-summer sophomore party, cut short when someone called the cops. Her mom handed her a twenty and told her that perhaps she'd like to pick up some aspirin while she was out getting the sandwiches.

Zoe rolled her eyes, snatched the twenty, and stuffed it into her tote. On her way out, her mom said something about her father and how she was so much like him.

How many times had Zoe heard that fearful tone in her mother's voice? And as hurtful as that remark was, it didn't sting nearly as much as the "why can't you be more like your sister?" line.

I'm nothing like my dad, Zoe reminded herself as she stepped out of Lacey's Herb and Flower Shoppe into dry heat and sunshine.

Pedestrians weaved in and out of eateries, a few taking the time to dine outside. Some hustled down the sidewalk, lunch in hand. Time seemed an inconvenience to some, a treasure to others.

A few tourists wandered up and down the sidewalk on the main street, cameras in hand, perhaps to capture Avalon's eclectic mix of Victorian and art deco architecture. The snow-capped Rocky Mountains and clear blue sky provided the perfect backdrop for any photographer.

Zoe ran across the street, barely missing an approaching car. The driver gently honked. She waved apologetically before stepping onto the sidewalk. *Safe!*

The doors of the shops and cafés were swung open wide, welcoming locals and tourists alike. As she approached the Abyss Bookstore, something caught her attention: a young guy reading poetry. His voice sounded confident, dramatic, and arrogant. Time took a hold of her. Curiosity got the best of her. The hangover cure would have to wait.

She stepped inside and casually leaned against the back wall, the coolness of the brick penetrating her thin black shirt. The ceiling fans, lazily spinning, circulated a sensuous breeze throughout, a breeze that carried a musty, woodsy scent.

On a small, round platform stood Poetry Guy. He was tall, slender. His dark, straight hair hung over his even darker eyes.

Then methought the air grew denser, perfumed from an unseen censer,
Swung by seraphim whose footfalls tinkled on the tufted floor.
"Wretch," I cried, "thy God hath lent thee—by these angels he hath sent thee."

He stopped reading and glanced up at her, a glance that lasted longer than it should have. His eyes were intense, yet lively, and she felt her face becoming hot. Was she blushing? She didn't think so. But what she did know was that her stomach was growling and her head was pounding.

She quickly left, ran into the deli, grabbed the sandwiches, thanked Mr. Petrelli, then headed back to the shop.

She plopped the sandwiches down on the checkout counter.

"What took you so long?" her mom asked, wheeling in a dolly stacked four boxes high.

"A poetry read at the Abyss."

"Poetry? Since when are you into poetry?"

"It wasn't the poetry I was interested in."

Her mother looked at her with raised eyebrows.

Zoe glanced over at the boxes. "New inventory?"

"A shipment of fairies," her mom replied.

"Fairies?" Zoe grabbed the top box. "Can I get started on these?"

Her mom held up the sandwiches. "After lunch."

Zoe practically inhaled her sandwich, then chased it all down with the energy drink. She let out a long, loud belch. Her mother gave her *the look*.

"I'll be in the back working on a flower arrangement if you need anything," her mom said, taking her half-eaten sandwich with her.

Feeling much better, Zoe started in on that first box. She carefully pulled out a fairy and stared, in awe of her beauty. Iridescent wings of purple swept above her head, long auburn hair swirled around her shoulders, and a gown of gold shimmered to her toes. And her face, so peaceful and joyful, gazed upon a hummingbird resting in her palm.

Zoe contemplated asking her mom if she could have her. But she would probably say no. Zoe already had a huge collection of fairies, elves, and angels. She'd open her bedroom window, lie in bed, and look up at the fairies, elves, and angels dangling from the ceiling, swaying in the breeze. Sometimes she'd light jasmine incense, but then her sister, Nicole, would yell at her for stinking up the whole upstairs.

"Better than your stupid perfumes!" Zoe would yell back. "And why don't you just smear on bug repellant?"

She couldn't wait to take out another fairy. Was it possible that the next one would be even more beautiful? Before she could find out, a delicate crash and a guy's soft "shit" broke her out of her spell.

She grabbed the handy little dustpan and brush from under the counter.

"Sorry about that," the guy said, staring at the pieces. "I guess I pulled a Jim."

"A what?" she asked, kneeling to sweep up the white porcelain pieces of what once was a unicorn with a now detached golden horn.

"You know, Jim, from *The Glass Menagerie*. He . . . never mind." He knelt down to help.

"I'll get it," she said. "It's my fault." She brushed the last of the pieces into the dustpan. "I'm supposed to put breakables farther back on the shelf."

"I can pay for it."

"No worries." She looked up at him, his dark eyes looking back. "Hey, you're the poetry guy."

"And you're the girl who didn't stay long. Poetry's not your thing?"

She shrugged. "Not really."

And it was the way in which he slightly tilted his head, then glanced away, that made her wish she'd said, *I love poetry, and I love it more than partying, shopping, and even horror flicks.* But she hadn't. Sigh.

"Are you finding everything okay?" she asked.

He walked over to a bin of assorted fresh flowers, pulled out a bouquet of yellow tulips, and slipped a plastic wrapper over the dripping stems. "I'll take these."

She forced a smile. "Excellent choice."

Her mom had told her to be sure to tell the customers what a great selection they'd made. That one comment made the customer feel confident about their purchase, which made for fewer returns and, hopefully, a satisfied, repeat customer. Zoe hoped that he would be one very satisfied and very repeat customer.

"Are these for anyone special?" she asked, trying not to sound that interested in him or his response.

"They're for my mom."

"Oh, thank god."

"What?"

"Thank god for such beautiful flowers," she said cheerfully.

He smiled, and she thought his smile looked like a "you are one weird chick" smile. She felt like diving into the flower bin, but walked behind the counter instead. Close enough.

He reached into his front jean pocket and pulled out a bunch of scrunched up bills. "My mom's been laid off for a while," he said, straightening out the money, "but she finally got a job, so we're doing the celebration thing tonight."

"Nice." Zoe rang up the flowers, and when she handed him his receipt and change, she hoped that he didn't notice her hand shaking.

"Thanks." He leaned toward her. "And are you sure?" he asked, his voice a whisper.

"Huh?"

"About the unicorn."

"Oh, that. Yeah, I'm sure." She started to close the cash drawer, but it stuck and beeped. She shoved it. It beeped even louder.

Her mom called out from the back room, "Hit the button on the side, Zoe."

She pushed the button, and the drawer sprung out like a snake about to bite her. Then, as if by magic, it closed. She breathed a sigh of relief and tucked a purple strand of hair behind her ear.

"Zoe?" he asked. "Zoe Weber?"

She wasn't sure she wanted to admit to her own identity.

"From Rock Ridge High?" he asked.

Now she really wasn't sure she wanted to admit who she was, and for a minute, she contemplated saying no.

But before she could give any answer, he continued, "The Zoe Weber who circulated a petition to stop frog dissection? The Zoe Weber who got caught smoking weed in the boys' bathroom? The Zoe Weber who had her art piece taken down at the art show because it was too—"

"It wasn't too anything," she blurted out. "It was a case of infantile censorship."

He looked at her and grinned. "So, you *are* that Zoe."

"How do you know about all that?"

"We went to the same high school."

"We did?"

He nodded.

"And you are?"

"Dylan. Dylan Foreman."

"I don't remember you."

"You probably don't remember me because I didn't stay."

She looked at him with a questioning glance.

"I didn't go back after Christmas break," he said. "I left to work full time at the bookstore." He shifted uncomfortably from one foot to the other. "So, you been working here long?"

But there was no way she was going to explain that she wasn't really just working, but paying off a fine—a fine handed down to her for underage drinking, curfew violation, and having had just a teeny weenie bit of weed. In the courtroom, the judge had appeared headless, and she was certain that it wasn't because she'd shown up for court stoned, but because his alabaster skin blended so perfectly into the beige wall behind him. She had snickered, but the sharp jab of her mother's bony elbow had jerked her back to reality. She winced all over at the memory.

"You okay?" he asked.

"Yeah," she said. "Anyway, I've been working here since school let out."

"It's a nice place," he said, glancing around.

Zoe thought so, and thought it was way cool that he thought so too. Her mom had bought the shop shortly after the divorce from her dad, a shop to keep her mom's mind occupied with the beautiful things in life when other things in life didn't seem so beautiful.

Being surrounded by the scent of essential oils, flowers, and herbs was perhaps as close to heaven on earth as she was ever going to get, or as close to heaven as she was going to get, period. Even if the cash register did jam while she was talking to a cute guy.

"Zoe, call Lisa Salisbury and tell her that her flower arrangement is ready," her mom said as she returned from the back room.

Zoe jumped at the sound of her mom's voice.

"Sorry," her mom said, glancing at Dylan. "I didn't know you were with a customer."

"Just finishing up," Zoe said, wishing her mom had better timing.

Her mom placed the bouquet on the mahogany accent table behind the checkout counter, and the scent of freshly cut red roses perfumed the air. She fussed and fussed with the white ribbon adorning the vase.

"I'll make sure it's perfect before Lisa comes in to pick it up," Zoe said.

"She spends a lot of money here," her mom said.

"I know," Zoe said, rolling her eyes.

Her mom gave the ribbon one last tug before returning to the back room.

"I got to go," Dylan said. "It was nice seeing you again, Zoe Weber."

"Thanks, and come again," she said.

He gave the flowers a little wave over his shoulder as he headed out.

She watched him leave. His gait was a bit cocky, but nice, and for some inexplicable reason, she liked him.

When she picked up the phone on the mahogany table to call Lisa, the mirror above it caught her reflection, and she couldn't help but wonder what Dylan saw when he looked at her. Did he think she was fat? She poked at her chipmunk cheeks and wondered if they would ever go away.

"He sure seemed like a nice young man," her mom said, setting a bouquet of pink calla lilies on the counter.

"Nice? He's hot."

"Remember the rules," her mom said. "No dating the customers."

"That didn't work with you and Charles."

Lacey's Herb and Flower Shoppe was on Charles's mail route. Sometimes he brought her mom a cup of steaming cappuccino from the coffeehouse across the street. Sometimes he stayed long enough to have a cup with her. Zoe never gave him much attention until that one day when Charles leaned over the counter and wiped whipped cream from the side of her mom's mouth and her mom giggled like her friends giggled whenever a boy showed even a little interest.

Within the year, her mom and Charles St. John were married. Zoe often wondered why her mom hadn't married someone like Charles to begin with and saved them all a lot of grief.

Chapter Two

Zoe unpacked the last box of fairies and positioned them on the glass display shelves. She rang up customers, took phone orders for fresh flower deliveries, and thought of Dylan only a few times, or maybe more than a few times. Okay, perhaps most of the day. She hadn't remembered him from school, but she smiled at the thought of him remembering her.

She filled three crystal vases with English lavender—which had been her grandmother's favorite herb—tied a purple ribbon around each one, then set them in the huge front display window. She added fairies on swings, and elves on bridges, and three large porcelain angels.

She stepped outside and, from a shopper's perspective, scrutinized the colors, textures, shapes, and symmetry. The display seemed to be suffocating. The objects needed more space between them. Everyone and everything needed space. Then she felt it, a strange sensation. She slowly turned and glanced toward the Abyss Bookstore, and there was Dylan, placing books and magazines in his own front window. He held up his hand and waved.

She wondered if he had been watching her the whole time—not that she minded. She gave a slight wave before stepping back inside. She grabbed one of the angels and pulled it up and over a vase, taking her eyes off the angel for only a moment to glance toward the bookstore. And then a deafening ting of porcelain hitting crystal echoed throughout the shop.

"Damn it!"

Her mother called out from the storeroom, asking if everything was all right, and Zoe called back that it was all good as she ran to grab the brush and dustpan. The ringing of the phone delayed her intentions. She took a deep breath before answering it.

"Lacey's Herb and Flower Shoppe."

"Do you sell good luck charms?" a guy asked.

"Yes, we do."

"Do they really work?"

"Well," she said, twirling the phone cord between her fingers, "I guess that depends on whether or not you believe in that sort of thing."

"Do you? Believe in charms? Believe in magic?"

"Ah, who is this?" she asked, shifting the phone to her other ear.

"I was just messing with you. It's me, Dylan. From the bookstore."

"Oh, hi," Zoe said, sounding as though she knew it was him all along. "So, you want to buy a lucky charm?"

"I might need one."

"For what?"

"For when I ask this girl out."

Her heart dropped. She felt like telling him to go find his good luck charm somewhere else and was about to hang up when he asked what she was doing that night. Her heart found its way back, but only for a moment. Not only was her mother adamant about her not dating the customers, but she was still grounded.

"I have plans," she blurted out.

"Oh."

The way he had said, "Oh," made her unsure that he believed her. "You could stop in tomorrow around three," she said, remembering that her mom would be leaving the shop around that time for a flower delivery, giving her plenty of time to spend with him.

"I'd like that," he said.

"Perfect. Then I'll see you tomorrow."

***

Zoe freshened up her lips with her favorite lip gloss, Cherry Blossom, then plucked a sprig from a mint plant and chewed on it.

She glanced at the clock. It was almost three-thirty. He wasn't coming, and she wondered why she had ever thought he would. She busied herself by attaching price tags to new inventory, and each time the door chimed, she looked up expectantly. Hoping they didn't detect her sullen attitude, she hurried a few customers through their purchases.

She grabbed the watering can and poured fresh water into the flower bin. The flowers, looking a bit wilted, seemed to hold as much life in them right now as she did. Lost in her pity party, the door chimed again. She didn't bother to look up until she heard a familiar voice call her name.

Her heart skipped a beat as Dylan breezed in and greeted her with a wide smile. She felt awash in cool water, alive again. She wondered if he knew just how hot he looked in his indigo jeans and black T-shirt.

"So, what's that?" she asked, pointing to the book in his hands.

"I bring you a work by John Donne."

"Never heard of him."

"Have you heard the line, 'Death be not proud,' or 'No man is an island'?"

She nodded. "So, I do know this guy."

"You do," he said. "Allow me to read to you from Donne's *Devotions Upon Emergent Occasions, Meditation Seventeen.* He hopped up on the counter and began. "'Perchance he for whom this bell tolls may be so ill as that he knows not it tolls for him.'"

Zoe grabbed the feather duster and dusted the glass shelves and figurines, only half-listening. She turned to glance at him to see if he was looking at her. He wasn't.

"'All mankind is of one author, and is one volume, when one man dies, one chapter is not torn out of the book, but translated into a better language.'"

Zoe wondered what this Donne guy meant by all that. Part of her didn't care, but another part of her wanted to care because Dylan seemed to.

She turned and smiled at him, slightly tapping the feather duster against her leg. "That was beautiful," she said.

"You're getting dust on your pants," he said.

She looked at her pant leg. Gray dust bunnies were clinging to it. Awkward.

He hopped off the counter. "I have to go." He walked toward the door, and with his hand on the doorknob, he turned around. "I'm doing another poetry reading tomorrow at noon. I'll be reading a selection from *The Prophet* by Kahlil Gibran."

Zoe didn't dare ask who that was. Instead, she said, "Oh, yeah, sure. She's awesome."

He chuckled. "So, I'll see you tomorrow?"

She nodded, wondering what had amused him.

When Zoe joined the gathering crowd at the Abyss Bookstore the next day, she sat toward the back, eating her sandwich while she listened to Dylan read the first selected poem, "On Children." She felt the poem was beautiful and thought that it was the perfect poem for her mom and stepdad to read. After all, she wasn't rebellious, stubborn, but adventurous, a free-spirit. *So, let the arrow fly. Let me, be me. Please stop trying to make me be like you.* Lost in her thoughts, she didn't even realize that Dylan had stopped reading and was now standing at her table.

She looked up at him, her mouth full of bread and smoked turkey, a bit of mayonnaise on her chin.

"Here," he said, handing her the book. "Keep it."

All eyes were on her, and she felt only slightly awkward. She smiled, thanked him, then quickly wrapped up the rest of her sandwich and headed back to the shop. Between waiting on customers, she read the poems, "On Love," "On Friendship," and "On Pleasure." But she skipped the poems, "On Pain" and "On Death." She liked the works of Kahlil Gibran and now realized what had amused Dylan.

Over the next few days, he visited her at the shop. She tried to keep from giggling too much whenever her mom was around. Her mom reminded her that she didn't want her flirting with the customers, especially Dylan.

Her mom's first impression of Dylan gave way to a raised eyebrow, a questioning glance, and an aloof disposition. She had apparently decided that a high school dropout with that just-crawled-out-of-bed look was not the kind of young man she wanted her daughter seeing, customer or not.

Zoe defended his disheveled look as being the latest in thing, and she tried to defend his decision to drop out of school, but her words were cut short with that look from her mom. She didn't care what her mom thought. No one and nothing was going to stand in her way of seeing him.

Chapter Three

Zoe twirled the spaghetti noodles around her fork while contemplating how she was going to meet Dylan at the ice arena. No longer grounded for the rest of her life, she didn't have to sneak out, but she did have to come up with a plan that didn't include him. "Isabelle," she mumbled to herself.

Her mom looked up from helping her half brother, Christopher, dish up his spaghetti. "What?"

"I'm meeting Isabelle at the ice arena tonight," she said.

"Doesn't she play in the summer band series in the park on Wednesday nights?"

"Did I say Isabelle?" Zoe said. "I meant Hailey. Just Hailey and me."

Her stepfather, Charles, poured himself another glass of wine. "Ice skating. Never been, but sounds like fun for the whole family."

"The ice arena? Since when are you into ice skating?" Nicole asked before stuffing a forkful of spaghetti into her mouth.

"Hailey says it's a great workout," Zoe said. "It helps her run track."

Her sister eyed her suspiciously. How was it that her sister was always on to her, always seemed to know when she was up to something?

"We should all go," Charles said, patting his stomach and letting out a belch. "I could use a good workout after this meal."

"Yeah, we should," said Nicole, still eyeing Zoe.

Zoe gave her sister a piercing glare.

"Are you kidding?" her mom said. "And miss *Law & Order?*"

Zoe smirked at her sister.

Her mom told her that it had better not be a late night and that she'd better not show up at the shop the next morning with a hangover or with any indication that she'd been drinking.

"Still paying off that fine, huh?" Nicole said.

Zoe eyed her sister, Little Miss Perfect, who'd never been grounded in her life or summoned to appear in court ever. Little Miss Boring.

"Before ten!" were the last words Zoe heard from her mom before running out of the house and away from her family.

The arena was alive with kids laughing, yelling, and shouting and with adults laughing right along with them.

"Zoe! Over here!" Dylan yelled, waving.

She smiled and waved back.

Dylan skated around the arena before taking one big

leap, then falling hard. Zoe held her breath, but only for a moment before bursting out laughing.

"I meant to do that!" he yelled.

He got back up on his feet and skated toward her, coming to an abrupt sideways stop, sending a spray of ice flakes onto her face.

"I suppose you meant to do that too," she said, wiping away the cold spray.

"I did," he said.

"You're good, by the way, ass fall and all."

"Yeah, well, my first time."

"Really?"

"Ah, no."

Zoe shook her head and grinned.

"Your skates are waiting for you at the counter. Don't worry about the rental fee. I got it."

"You reserved a pair for me?" she asked, hoping he didn't detect the terror in her voice. "But I've never done this." She looked out over the arena. "There are so many kids out there."

"They're not going to bite you. Okay, maybe run over you with their sharp blades, but a little bit of blood is part of the action." He grinned and pointed to the counter.

Before she knew it, she was lacing up her skates. With trepidation, she stepped onto the ice. After a few "oh shits," a few "oh my gods," a slight slip, and an almost butt kiss to the ice, she'd had enough.

Dylan skated over to her. "Take my hand. We'll do this together."

She put one hand in his, and with the other gripping the rail, they began.

"I thought it would be easier than this," she said, walking more than skating.

"The pros always make it look easy."

They circled the arena a few times before she decided to try skating on her own. After about ten minutes of being on her butt more than her feet, she managed to stay up for a few awkward trips around the arena. She thought she was finally getting the hang of it and waved to Dylan to try to get his attention to tell him. She felt proud and happy, but then her body started leaning forward farther than she thought it should and her arms, as though possessed, made small, rapid circles. When she straightened back up, she overcompensated. Her butt hit the ice hard and a sharp chill surged straight up her spine.

Strong arms wrapped underneath hers and pushed her body forward and up. Before she knew it, she and Dylan were skating together, one of his hands on the small of her back, the other in hers. He smiled at her and held her close. It seemed so easy now. They rounded a corner, bodies in sync. But when his skate nicked hers, her legs and brain were no longer in sync. She reached for the rail, and just as she was about to fall, grabbed it.

Dylan slammed into her, and they both jerked forward. He quickly slid his arms under hers and grabbed hold of the rail, pressing firmly against her. She stopped wobbling.

He drew his lips close to her ear. "You okay?"

Her heart still pounding, she nodded.

He gently placed his hands on her waist, turned her around, leaned over, and kissed her. A gentle, warm kiss on the hard, cold ice. The warmth of the kiss drew deep into her and charged every cell in her body with a thousand tiny light bulbs and lightning bugs and fireworks and all those things, and was it her imagination, or did she just sink a fraction of an inch into the ice?

"Meet me later tonight," he whispered.

Chapter Four

After the house grew quiet, Zoe slipped out through the sliding glass door into the night. The air felt brisk and it chilled her. She zipped up her hoodie, then ran across the yard, crawled over the chain-link fence, and ran to the bottom of the hill. Dylan was leaning against the passenger side of his Jeep, smoking a cigarette. He took one last drag before tossing it to the curb.

A bit out of breath, she finally reached him and wrapped her arms around him, giving him a good squeeze. "So, where to?" she asked.

"I have this great place I'd like to take you," he said. "No questions."

"Whatever," she said. "I scored some weed by the way. I mean, if you're okay with that."

"Hell yeah. Right on."

Dylan opened her door, but not before giving her a quick kiss on the lips. He jumped in, then headed west on Highway 74 and into the canyons of the Rocky Mountains. Zoe reached into the pocket of her hoodie, pulled out a pipe, lit it, and passed it to Dylan.

"Can't you wait until we get there?" he asked lightheartedly.

"Which is where?"

"No questions."

After about fifteen minutes, Dylan veered off the highway onto a dirt road. They drove to a secluded, grassy area, surrounded by aspen and pine. He turned off the ignition.

"So this is it?" she asked. "The place you wanted me to see?"

"Look behind you."

She turned to look out the back window. City lights twinkled far below in the valley. She didn't have the heart to tell him that this was not the first time she'd been here.

"Wow, the view is totally amazing," she said.

"Told you this was a great place. There's a creek not far from here."

She knew that too.

He grabbed the blankets from the back, she grabbed the cooler, and together they headed toward the creek. She picked up the pace and took off running, laughing as she looked over her shoulder.

"Hey, wait up!" Dylan yelled as he ran after her. He grabbed the cooler as he overtook her and kept running.

When she caught up to him, she leapt onto his back. He lost his balance and fell to the ground, taking her with him. The cooler and the blankets went flying. He got to his feet and ran a few steps. She, half crawling, half running, grabbed his ankle and knocked him off balance again. Then she flung herself on top of him and straddled him.

"So, you think you're faster than me?" she asked.

"Well, maybe not faster, but definitely stronger." He flipped her over, straddled her, and grabbed her flailing arms, holding them down at the wrists.

She struggled against him. "Get off me you big—"

"Tell me how wonderful I am and I will," he said.

"What?"

"You heard me. Tell me how wonderful I am."

"You're wonderful."

"Not good enough."

"You're really, really wonderful."

"Come on, Zoe. You can do better than that."

"Okay, you're the most wonderful, kind, generous, sophisticated, intelligent, arrogant, obnoxious asshole a girl could ever ask for."

Dylan grinned. "That's more like it."

He flipped off her sandal and tickled her foot. She laughed and laughed, gasping for air and begging him to stop. He continued to run his fingers up and down the arch of her foot.

"Had enough?" he asked.

"Yes!"

"Okay, up you go." He helped her up and reached for her sandal. "Your slipper, Your Highness," he said, placing it on her foot.

She laughed. "Thank you, Prince of Cooler Snatching."

At the creek, he spread out a blanket and they plopped down, hip to hip. He wrapped the other blanket around their shoulders and opened a beer for each of them. She lit the pipe, took a hit, then passed it to him.

She leaned her head against his shoulder and looked up at the night sky. The full moon along with the residue of city lights created a sky of anemic twinkles. She knew that if she and Dylan wanted to see the stars in all their glory, they'd have to be much farther beyond the city limits.

"You want to go with me and my sister to Durango at the end of August to visit my dad?" she asked. "He'll probably be drunk . . . and stoned. Just pretend you don't notice."

"I can't."

"You can't pretend you don't notice?"

"I mean I have to help my mom get my little sisters ready for school," he said. "Maybe another time."

Zoe asked him about his family, and he told her about his sisters, his mom, and his dad. He told her that the day he came into the shop to buy the flowers for his mom wasn't just because his mom had gotten a job, but because they were also no longer homeless.

"About six months," he answered when Zoe asked him for how long.

Zoe felt stupid now that she had even asked. Homeless was homeless. What did time have to do with it?

"No worries," he said.

When he got to the story of his dad, she felt sad. Drunk driving. Two years ago. One moment here. Another moment gone. Soon after, his world unraveled.

"I'm sorry," she said, tenderly squeezing his hand.

Her heart felt heavy with words, but she grew silent. What words could she say? He had lost his dad and she still had hers. There were times when she had wished she didn't have her dad, that he were dead. Now she felt terrible.

She shivered.

Dylan snuggled closer to her, wrapping the blanket tighter around them.

"Look," she said, pointing toward the sky. "The Big Dipper." She traced the stars with her finger, drawing it into the space before them. "The stars aren't like this outside Durango. There they seem so close, like you can almost reach out and grab one."

"When you get there," he said, "reach out, grab one, and make a wish."

"What wish do you want?"

"Make it for you," he said. "I've already got mine."

He kissed her, a tender and perfect kiss. He pulled the blanket up and over them and she felt herself melting into him and into the softness of the night, into the darkness of the night.

***

Zoe groggily sat up and rubbed her eyes. She squinted toward the horizon, a hint of orange light glimmered. Her head pounded and she wished she'd taken a few aspirin the night before or at least brought some with her.

Lightweight.

Light!

Wait!

She reached over and shook Dylan. "Dylan. Wake up. Wake up!"

He mumbled something.

"Get up!" she said.

She grabbed her pipe and weed, stuffed them into her

pocket, then threw the beer cans into the cooler.

"Dylan, come on," she said, gently kicking at his hip.

He groaned, then staggered up. She quickly bundled up the blankets and tossed them to him. He was too busy rubbing his eyes to catch them.

"Dylan, a little help here, please," she said.

"My head hurts."

"More than your head is going to hurt if you don't get moving."

Once on the highway, Zoe looked out the window at the blur of the gray and brown and red of the land and the blur of the aspen and pine. The early morning hours seemed so quiet. Mist hung in the air. Dew blanketed the earth. Dylan seemed so quiet. Something didn't feel quite right as he sped down the curvy mountain highway. She glanced over at him. The same Dylan, who brought a smile to her face. Yet something was different, unsettling. But what? She looked back out across the hills rushing past.

So deep in her thoughts, she didn't even see it coming.

A sudden, violent jolt. Tires screeching, metal grating against metal, rubber burning, glass shattering, glass spraying, body-slam to the dash, body jerking back, then forward and forward even more, now weightless.

Frigid air.

Hard. Heavy. Slam.

Grass. Dirt. Blood.

Pain. Wretched pain.

The cold morning dew soaked through the front of her hoodie. The crisp mountain air penetrated to her bones.

Birds chirping. Swoosh of cars. Car doors slamming. Voices. Woman screaming. Sirens. Sirens growing louder, louder. High-pitched bleep. Then, silence.

Peace.

Quiet.

Gentle nothingness.

Zoe slowly pushed herself up from the damp earth. She stood, and for a moment, just stood there glancing around, a bit disoriented. She looked down at her jeans, covered in mud. She brushed off the mud, then turned and looked up toward the road.

Two paramedics rushed down the steep embankment toward her. She was about to call out to tell them that she was okay, but before she could get the words out they whisked past her. She followed them, wondering where they were going. She asked, but they didn't seem to hear her. She was about to ask again when the sight of a girl lying in an aspen grove stopped her.

That girl is wearing my hoodie.

The paramedics turned the girl over.

Oh my god that's . . .

A deafening static filled the space around her. She cupped her hands over her ears. *Turn that off!* But the sound wrapped around her, tighter and tighter. She felt her body being squeezed, then being sucked away from that girl wearing her hoodie, sucked away from the paramedics, sucked away from Dylan.

Chapter Five

Zoe floated and floated and floated, and the static slowly faded, and then, silence. Peace embraced her and Love wrapped around her, a love she had never felt before. The Love grew intense, to the point where she couldn't bear it. She told the Love, *too much, too much,* and the Love gently softened.

Another loud swoosh, then plush, warm grass snuggled her bare feet and tickled her toes. She found herself standing on a cliff overlooking a vibrant field of lavender swaying in an emerald valley, and the lavender glowed luminous shades of purples and blues and pinks, glowing as though breathing in and out with the ebb and flow of life.

A light, gentle breeze tickled her face, blowing the scent of the lavender to her and seemingly saying, "Come, delight in me as I delight in you."

But how will I get down from the cliff?

In that thought, Zoe found herself standing in the middle of the emerald valley in the field of lavender. The flowers swayed in the breeze, tickling her bare legs. The softness of the earth wrapped around her feet, and she giggled in delight. The earth giggled back. The breeze playfully blew through her hair, and the softness of the wind tickled her face. She laughed and the wind laughed back.

In the distance, she saw a woman with long, shimmering silver hair and glowing skin. The woman smiled the most brilliant, peaceful smile. Zoe thought she recognized her. She did recognize her!

"Grandma!"

Her grandmother's arms wrapped around her, holding her tightly. Zoe hugged her back. She didn't think she'd ever want to let go. When she felt her grandmother pull away, Zoe held fast. She wanted to stay this way forever. Her grandmother gently released their embrace and smiled, and in that smile, Zoe felt a deep and profound love, an intense, immeasurable love. She felt lighter. So much lighter.

Lavender brushed against her bare legs as though saying hello. She skimmed her hand along the lavender and the flowers glowed an even brighter purple.

"Look at my hands, Grandma. They're glowing purple, like the lavender."

Her grandmother smiled at her as though saying, You haven't seen anything yet.

"It's so beautiful here. I never thought a world could hold such beauty. I feel cheated now."

"What good would this beauty hold for you if you had always known of it? Beauty and knowledge. Knowledge and beauty."

"Knowledge? What does knowledge have to do with beauty. With anything here?"

"Come." Her grandmother reached out her hand. "Let me show you."

Zoe took her grandmother's hand in hers. It felt so soft, smooth, plump. She looked at her grandmother's hand. It looked nothing like it had when she was in hospice. Gone were the protruding blue veins and the dark brown spots and the spots that looked like bruises.

Zoe looked up at her and smiled.

They walked along a cobbled path, then over a wooden footbridge to a verdant meadow alive with a sea of purple irises, yellow daffodils, and orange poppies, none of which clung close to the earth, but stood tall, almost five feet tall, as though they had anticipated Zoe's arrival and had risen to greet her. She brushed her fingers over the soft petals and breathed in the sweet floral scent and immediately felt blissfully intoxicated.

Something flew around her, and she let go of her grandmother's hand and followed the winged creature. She chased it until it fluttered around the purple irises. A bumblebee?

Hummingbird?

Dragonfly?

Zoe took a closer look.

A fairy!

The fairy looked up at her, winked, and waved her wand over the irises before buzzing off to the poppies. Zoe looked closely at the flowers. Fairies hovered over all of them, waving their wands and spreading fragrance throughout the meadow.

She looked up at her grandmother. "Is this what you

meant by beauty and knowledge? That fairies really do exist?"

The only answer her grandmother gave her was a smile, and Zoe watched as her grandmother raised her hand and pushed it back as though opening a huge curtain. Zoe looked straight ahead, her eyes widening at the view slowly appearing before her, and in that moment, she wondered if those poppies had anything to do with what she was now seeing.

In the distance stood an edifice of bright gold shimmering before her like sunlight reflecting off cascading water. Diamonds and emeralds and rubies and sapphires trimmed the arched doors, and the only value they held was the value of Beauty. The arched doors slowly opened to reveal a crystal building.

"Are we going in there?"

Before Zoe heard the answer, she and her grandmother passed through the large arched doors and into a room, a room full of scrolls and nothing but scrolls.

Zoe looked at her grandma. "No Internet?"

Her grandmother laughed. "This is better than the Internet, and these scrolls aren't just any scrolls. They're magic."

"Is this the knowledge you were talking about?"

She nodded. "So, what are you dying to know? No pun intended."

Zoe laughed, but before she could answer, she felt her body being pulled toward the scrolls. She floated closer and closer until she could actually see the writing. It was not in

a language she understood, and yet she was able to decipher
it.

"Math? Ugh. I would have to end up in this section."

A strong tug and a sharp jolt like a circuit passed through
her, and soon after, mathematical equations and formulas
appeared in front of her like a hologram. The numbers,
symbols, and letters appeared to dance before her, and then
they passed through her. She turned around. They continued to dance around and through her, and in the dance, she
understood all of it. Math. Easy. Simple. Fun. Imagine that.

She felt the circuit release, and then a soft tug.

Music.

Beings of glowing light surrounded her, singing a most
glorious song, and for each note, a different hue emanat-
ed from each being. She felt as though the music passed
through her, and now the music was inside of her, breathing for her, and filling her up with life. Zoe listened and
listened and listened.

She floated through the Crystal Palace and through all
its glorious colors. She swam into yellow and felt warmth.
Blue felt cool. Pink tickled. Red felt invigorating. Green was
happy. Purple glorious. Gold joyous. All of the colors tasted
as sweet as the sweetest honey and felt as soft as the softest
feather.

Then something pulled and tugged at her, but this wasn't
like the tug of the scrolls. This felt unnerving and scary, like
moving through water with weights attached to her ankles
and wrists.

She looked down. Her grandmother was standing in the

lavender field, waving to her. Zoe waved back. Her grand-mother continued waving. Zoe felt a stronger tug. She didn't like the feeling. She resisted. She moved her arms and legs to stay afloat, but her body continued to feel weighted down. She kept moving, but she wasn't going anywhere.

Suddenly, her body stopped.

Then,

falling,

falling,

falling.

Kerplunk.

The deep emerald grass tickled her face. This time she didn't feel like giggling. She wanted to go back to the music, to the colors, even to the scrolls on math. She wanted to keep on floating and floating and floating. Her heart ached for that beauty, for that peaceful bliss.

She stood and looked at her grandmother, and the two of them just stood there, looking at one another. Whatever her grandmother was about to say, Zoe wasn't too sure she wanted to hear it. And then her grandmother spoke the words: "Zoe, you can't stay."

The words stung Zoe's heart.

"But Grandma, I want to. I want to stay here with you. Please."

"There's no time. Come."

"But—"

"Now, child!"

Her grandmother grabbed Zoe's hand with a firm grip. A surge of fear swept through her. They quickly walked across the meadow to the footbridge. Zoe grew even more fearful. This was happening too fast. She wanted to go back. She wanted to go back and see the Crystal Palace again, be in the Crystal Palace again, but Grandma quickened her pace. Zoe struggled to keep up. She had to see the palace. At least one more time. She glanced over her shoulder. It was gone! The Crystal Palace was gone!

How is that possible? It was just there. Grandma must have closed that curtain.

Her grandmother's grip grew even tighter and her pace even quicker as they stepped onto the footbridge.

Why is Grandma in such a hurry? "Slow down, Grandma. Please don't rush me."

They were almost to the end of the bridge when her grandmother finally slowed her pace. Zoe hoped her grandmother had slowed because she now realized she had made a mistake, a terrible mistake, and that they did have to go back to the Crystal Palace and that she would make it reappear.

But her grandmother stopped and stood still, eerily still. She looked into the distance with a faraway look that seemed to take in everything, yet nothing.

She turned her gaze back to Zoe, and the love in her grandmother's eyes washed over her, showering her with rays of peace.

Her grandmother placed her hands on Zoe's cheeks.

"There are things you must do, my dear. They need you."

"Who needs me?"

But before she got her answer, her grandmother floated away. Zoe reached out to pull her back, but she couldn't move, and it was as though an invisible shield separated them, and the distance between them grew farther, farther, farther until her grandmother disappeared.

Zoe stood on the footbridge alone, terribly alone, and in her aloneness she grew frightened. She started walking across the bridge. Why did the bridge seem to stretch out to eternity? Her walk turned into a run. The bridge stretched and stretched and stretched before her. Would she never reach the end?

She ran and ran and ran, finally reaching the end, where she leapt off and flew through the air, and upon landing, her feet sunk into the cool softness of the plush grass. She sank a bit more and more and even more and she wondered if she was ever going to stop sinking. She willed herself to stop, and in that desire she heard an earsplitting, high-pitched scratchy screechy mess of a sound. Then, silence, and the silence comforted her and cocooned her. A delicate scent of lavender surrounded her.

Where am I?

Stainless steel. White walls. Bright, big round lights.

Blurry figures moved before her, slowly, methodically, as though swimming underwater. A blue cap covered their heads and a blue mask their mouths. Eyes. She could only see their eyes. The figures leaned over a table.

Zoe heard a high-pitched, steady sound. She looked at a screen. A straight line moved across it. The figures stepped away from the table. A nurse pulled back a blue drape to reveal a nude, whitish-gray body. Another nurse applied paddles to the chest. The body rose grotesquely off the table and fell with a thud. Again. The body rose. The body fell.

Thud. Again. The monitor blipped and bleeped and a line jagged across the screen.

She walked toward the table and as she drew closer, it seemed as though the figures sensed her presence and parted, allowing her to pass by them. Closer, closer she walked toward the table. She reached the table and looked at the body.

Purple, swollen eyes.

Cut, swollen lip.

Blood-stained skin.

Blood-matted hair.

Loud. Deafening. *Swoosh!*

Cold.

Damp.

Heavy.

Confined.

Squished.

Grandma, where are you?

Chapter Six

Zoe felt the soft touch of someone's hand on her arm, another softly stroking her head. Delicate notes of citrus perfumed the air. Someone sniffled. Someone whispered. Someone softly sang.

Zoe stirred. "Grandma, Grandma."

"Dad, she's waking up," Christopher said. He climbed down from his father's lap and walked over to her bedside. "Hi Zoe, Zoe. Hi Zoe, Zoeee. Hieee," he said in his sing-songy voice.

Someone squeezed her hand. "Hey, Zoe, it's me, Mom. We're all here."

Zoe slowly opened her eyes. Her mom looked blurry.

"You gave us quite a scare," Charles said, standing now next to Christopher.

He looked blurry too.

"Hey, Zoe."

Was that her sister's voice? She sounded like she'd been crying. Had she been crying?

Zoe moaned. "It was so beautiful."

Charles leaned over the bed. "What did you say, Zoe?"

"Grandma said I couldn't stay."

"What's she saying, Dad?" Christopher asked.

"Nothing, son. She's tired. She's just tired."

Zoe reached her hand out to Charles. "Home. I want to go back home."

Christopher stroked Zoe's arm. "You can't go home yet, Zoe. You have to get much, much better, and after you get much, much better then you can come home, but you have to stay here for a really, really, really long time and—"

"Christopher, that's enough," Charles said, placing his hand on his son's shoulder.

Christopher patted Zoe's cheek. "I sorry, Zoe."

"I want Grandma," she mumbled.

Charles leaned in closer. "Zoe, do you know where you are? You're in the hospital. You were in a very bad car accident. We're all here for you."

"Grandma too?"

"No, Zoe," Charles said. "Your grandmother is not here. Nicole, Christopher, your mom, and I are here."

Silence.

"Zoe?"

***

Life seemed so quiet. Too quiet. Except for that beeping. Zoe wondered if those beeps had something to do with her. She strained to sit up, but her body denied her.

Footsteps pitter-pattering, and shortly thereafter, drapes swishing open. Bright sunlight fell upon Zoe's face. She squinted at the painful brightness and pulled the blanket up to cover her eyes.

Someone gently pulled the blanket away. "I know you're too old for peek-a-boo, honey, and I know you'd love to stay in that comfortable, warm bed, but we need to get you up and walking."

"Walking?"

The nurse nodded.

Zoe reached up and touched her throat. "What's this?"

"It's a soft cervical collar. It'll help keep your head movement to a minimum while your neck injury heals."

"Neck injury?"

"You'll have to wear it for a few weeks." The nurse sat down on the edge of the bed. "You got real lucky, young lady."

She began to peel a bandage from Zoe's forehead.

Zoe winced.

"It's almost off, honey."

Zoe looked at the nurse's nametag. "Sierra Juliette. That's a pretty name."

"Thank you. Named after my grandma."

"Grandma's are wonderful."

"They sure are," Sierra said. "Okay, done. Now come on. We need to get you out of that bed."

"My grandma took me to the most incredible place."

Sierra put her arms around Zoe. "Lean on me and I'll lift you."

"It was so beautiful."

"Well, if you want to go back there, we have to get you up and moving."

"Grandma said I couldn't go back. I had things to do here."

"She got that right. Like walking. Now come on. Lean on me."

Zoe grunted and leaned on Sierra, and before her brain could sync up with her mouth, she blurted out, "I love you."

"I love you too," Sierra said, matter-of-factly.

The last time she'd blurted out an "I love you" was to her sister at two o'clock in the morning, but it was more like, "I wuuuv youuu," and a few octaves higher than normal. Her sister had said, "Wherever you are, I hope you have the common sense to stay there," and, "Do I need to come get you?"

Zoe braced herself against Sierra's soft, warm, and generously built body, but as soon as her feet hit the floor, her knees buckled and her body began to slither to the floor.

"I gotcha, baby," Sierra said, wrapping her strong, fleshy arms around Zoe's waist. "But you're not going anywhere without me or that."

A walker?

Sierra helped Zoe shuffle over to it.

"I only walked a few feet," she said, "and I'm already tired. I feel like I'm dying. Am I dying?"

"No, baby, you're not dying," Sierra said. "You've come through the worst of it and you're going to be fine. It's going to take some time, though."

"I have to pee."

Sierra helped Zoe shuffle into the bathroom and told her she'd be right outside the door should she need her.

She shuffled toward the toilet, but caught her reflection in the mirror. She felt paralyzed with shock and disbelief, and a fog clouded her mind, taking away her ability to sense who that person was staring back at her.

My god, I look like a boxer who's lost a fight. Or maybe won.

Her eyes were swollen, one almost completely shut. A gash zigzagged down her forehead and across to where an eyebrow had once been. She leaned in closer.

Her knees grew weak, weaker, her whole body trembling now. She reached for the sink to steady herself, but her hand slid over the rim. Her hand in the air now, nothing to hang onto, nothing to brace herself against. She tried to call for help, but the words got all tangled up inside.

***

Zoe awoke to the worried looks of her mom and Charles.

"I'm ugly."

Mom took Zoe's hand and assured her that the swelling would go down.

"My forehead."

"It'll heal."

"I can't even hardly walk."

"Eventually you will."

And when her mom had told her that eventually she would walk again, Zoe hadn't realized that it would be so soon.

The following afternoon, Sierra placed the walker in front of Zoe and ordered her up.

Zoe groaned. "You sure were a lot nicer yesterday."

"Sorry, baby, but walking is the best thing for you."

Sierra linked her arm in Zoe's and helped her grab hold of the walker. After steadying herself, Zoe shuffled her way out of the room, and with Sierra by her side, began her walk down a very long corridor, a corridor that appeared endless.

Within a few days, Zoe graduated from the walker to a cane. She asked Sierra, "Will I always walk with a limp?"

"Probably," Sierra said. "But you're going to recover just fine. Eventually, you won't even need the cane."

"What about this?" Zoe asked, pointing to the scar that zigzagged down her forehead and across her eyebrow.

Sierra shook her head. "That will always be there to serve as a constant, gentle reminder of the warrior in you."

Warrior.

Zoe liked how that word sounded, how that word felt, and she decided right then that perhaps having a scar wouldn't be so bad after all.

***

Sierra wheeled Zoe to the exit, and once outside, Zoe thanked her and gave her a hug good-bye. Charles thanked her, too, for taking such good care of "his baby." Zoe told Sierra that she wasn't really the baby, that Christopher was, but Sierra told Zoe that no matter how old she got, she'd always be her father's baby. And Zoe liked the sound of that. But she liked the sound of "warrior" better.

Charles held the front passenger door open for her, and she rose from her wheelchair, steadying herself with her cane, but as soon as she shuffled to the front seat, she stopped.

Charles looked at her. "Zoe, you can get in now. Zoe?"

"Charles?"

"Yes?"

"I want to sit in the back."

"The back? Okay, yeah, sure. You can sit in the back."

He helped her with her seat belt. Zoe looked up at him. Was that a tear forming?

As he drove out of the parking lot and onto the street, she kept catching his worried glimpses in the rearview mirror. She assured him she was comfortable, couldn't wait to get home, but could he slow down a bit? He eased off the gas. Better, much better.

"Charles?"

"Yes?"

"Is Dylan okay?"

A long pause. She wondered if perhaps he hadn't heard her. "He's okay, Zoe," he said. "Just a few cuts and scrapes."

Thank god.

"But your mom and I don't want you seeing him anymore."

But I have to.

She felt tired, so tired. She wasn't even sure if she had said that out loud, or if she had said it to herself. She felt delirious, drugged. She couldn't wait to get home and crawl into her bed. Her own bed for the first time in what seemed like such a long time. No more nurses and doctors to poke and prod her, or to wake her to take her temperature and blood pressure, or to help her to the bathroom. No more being told to walk, walk, and walk some more.

And no more hospital food.

The collar would eventually be removed, her limp would lessen, and the scar across her forehead would heal and leave the only trace of the car accident. Or so she thought.

Charles pulled into the driveway. "Hold on. I'll get your door."

"Thanks, Charles."

He opened the door and reached in to help her. "I got you, Zoe."

"I want to do it myself," she said, grabbing her cane.

And she did. Slow, steady shuffles to the front door, her stepdad following her every step. Once inside, the sound of familiar voices said, "Welcome home, Zoe!"

A Welcome Home banner hung across the arched entrance to the dining room, balloons floated toward the ceiling, and on the dining room table were platters of food. So much food. And her favorite, a chocolate cake. A huge bouquet of bright pink stargazer lilies mixed with deep purple irises was on the table, along with a teddy bear and cards. Lots of cards. She wanted to say thank you, but she got so choked up, all she could do was smile.

Her mom and Nicole greeted her with hugs. Her aunt Maggie greeted her with a warm embrace, and her soft, dark curls brushed against Zoe's face, tickling her cheek. A few neighbors; her two best friends, Hailey and Isabelle; and an aunt and uncle on her stepdad's side were all there to welcome her home. And so many hugs. Her mom telling all of them to be careful. "Don't hug too tight." "She's got that neck collar on for a reason." "She's still bruised and sore." "Watch the cane."

"You look great," Hailey said.

"Liar," Zoe said.

"Yeah, you look like shit," Hailey said, giving her a gentle hug.

"We're so glad you're okay," Isabelle said. "We sure missed you."

"Nice scar," Hailey said.

"Thanks."

"Will it always look like that?" Isabelle asked.

"Pretty much."

"You can always grow your hair out over it and maybe nobody will notice," Hailey said.

"What about that cane?" Isabelle asked. "Will you always have to use that? And that thing around your neck. What's up with that?"

"Zoe," her mom asked, "would you like something to eat?"

And before she could answer, Aunt Maggie said, "I'll fix her a plate."

Christopher skipped up to Zoe. "Can I play with your cane?" he asked. "You can play with my balloon." He extended his bright red balloon to her, which read Get Well Soon.

The room seemed to be closing in, the air stifling. So many people, too many questions. She leaned heavily into her cane with a downward, blank gaze.

"Zoe?" her mom asked. "Are you okay?"

"I just want to go to my room." She wrapped her arms around Christopher and hugged him. "You can play with my cane later."

"We'll help her, Mrs. Weber," Hailey said. "Come on, Isabelle."

Hailey and Isabelle shuffled along with Zoe to her bedroom, then quietly shut the door.

"Do you want us to get you anything?" Hailey asked while helping Zoe into bed.

"Zoe?"

"Fairies are real," she said.

"What?" Hailey said.

"Fairies. They're real. I saw them"

"You saw fairies?" Isabelle asked, slowly looking up toward the ceiling at the many fairies dangling there. She looked back at Zoe. "In a dream, you mean?"

"It was in a place like heaven," Zoe said. "But it wasn't heaven."

Hailey and Isabelle exchanged glances.

"Zoe, are you sure you don't want us to get you anything," Hailey asked, "like some water or something?"

"It was so incredible. So peaceful. Nothing like here." Zoe strained to sit up, but winced in pain. She relaxed into the softness of her pillow. She told them about the field of flowers and the fairies who waved their wands, spreading the scent.

"That's quite some dream," Hailey said.

"It wasn't a dream."

"Fine, it wasn't a dream," said Isabelle. "I don't want to hear about fairies, anyway. I want to hear about what happened."

"We overheard your mom and your aunt talking about some guy you were with," Hailey said.

"Who was he, Zoe?" Isabelle asked.

"His name's Dylan," Zoe said.

"Why didn't you tell us about him?" Isabelle asked.

Zoe proceeded to tell her two best friends all about Dylan from school.

"I think I remember him," Hailey said. "Tall guy, dark?"

Zoe nodded.

"Kind of mysterious and arrogant?" Hailey asked.

"I guess so," Zoe said.

"Kind of an ass sometimes?" Hailey asked.

Zoe looked confused now.

"I think we had detention together once," Hailey said. "He read poetry, out loud, in detention. Totally against the rules."

"I remember that poetry-reading dude," Isabelle said. "That guy? You hooked up with the poetry dude?"

"Yeah," said Zoe.

"That guy was hot," Isabelle said.

"Totally," said Hailey.

Zoe struggled to find her voice. She had so much she wanted to tell them about Dylan, fairies, heaven, her grandma . . . but like an enemy cloaked in a scratchy black blanket, fatigue wrapped around her, sending her into a world of confusing and unsettling dreams.

Chapter Seven

Zoe slowly opened her eyes. Hailey? Isabelle? They were just here, weren't they? Maybe they had gone back into the living room or had gone home. She slowly got out of bed, reached for her cane, and yawned her way into the bathroom. She looked at her reflection in the mirror, something she hadn't wanted to do since that day her face hit the cold tile floor in the hospital.

She decided that she actually liked what she saw. She no longer looked like that boxer who had lost a fight, but a warrior who had won. But that scar across her forehead and a half-missing eyebrow distressed her. She pulled a comb from the drawer and combed her hair down over her forehead. She tugged at her purple highlights. In despair, she tossed the comb back into the drawer. Her mom's reflection appeared in the mirror, her hands outstretched, holding pills and a glass of water.

"How are you feeling?" her mom asked.

"Better, actually." She popped the painkiller and the muscle relaxant and downed the glass of water. "Where is everybody?"

"Zoe, it's almost noon."

"Noon? I've been sleeping all this time?"

Her mom nodded. "Do you want something to eat?"

She did, and after eating, she was back in bed. And that was the extent of Zoe's life during her first week home: eat, sleep, bathroom, repeat. But it wasn't long before she felt the warrior within rise up. Soon, she was strong enough to go outside, cane in hand, and take short walks with her mom by her side. She loved getting out of the house into the fresh air, but those walks exhausted her, and after eating more creamed spinach and creamed corn, and creamed whatever-her-mom-could-cream-for-her, she was back in bed.

She looked forward to the day when her throat wasn't so swollen and she could eat something other than easy-to-chew, easy-to-swallow foods. She looked forward to the day when she could walk without her cane, when the scar was less visible, when the soft cervical collar was removed, when she was back to partying with her friends. She looked forward to the day when her life was normal again, even if normal meant predicable and boring. And, she looked forward to the day when she was with Dylan.

***

Zoe limped into the kitchen and into the scent of basil and oregano. Her mother stood at the stove stirring a pot of marinara sauce.

"Smells and looks good, Mom, but what culinary delight have you planned for me this evening?" she asked.

"You are having applesauce, mashed potatoes, creamed peas, and tapioca pudding," she said.

Zoe laughed. "That all sounds so much better than your homemade cooking."

"It's good to see you haven't lost your sense of humor." She grabbed the applesauce from the refrigerator. "Heated or cold?"

"Heated with a bit of cinnamon, please."

Her mom popped the applesauce into the microwave. "But I don't think you'll find any humor in what's on the kitchen table."

Zoe glanced over at the table. An envelope. She picked it up and pulled out a letter. She scanned it over. Drug paraphernalia. In her possession. Summoned to appear in court. She stared at the letter in disbelief. How could they do that? Didn't they understand what she had just gone through? What she's continuing to go through? She almost died, for god's sake. Okay, as far as she was concerned, she did die. Couldn't they have realized how bad off she was and forgive this little incident?

I think I just got grounded for the rest of my life.

The microwave beeped four times as though saying, "No shit," followed by two exclamation marks.

"Mom, does Charles know?"

"Not yet," Mom said, stirring cinnamon into the applesauce.

"When are you going to tell him?"

Her mom stopped and looked at her daughter. "I'm not. You are. And don't put that letter in some convenient spot for him to find."

Zoe devised a plan. She would show him the letter after dinner, not before, because showing it to him before would upset him and he wouldn't be able to eat and he'd be grumpy throughout the entire meal. She would slide the letter over to him, tell him she was tired and needed her medication, and then she'd go straight to bed. And when he came into her room to confront her, she'd pretend to be asleep.

She folded the letter back up and tucked it into the pocket of her sweatpants. She knew Charles would not be happy with her going back to court, for the second time in three months no less, but at least this time she had vulnerability on her side.

After Charles said grace, Zoe looked at her plate of applesauce, mashed potatoes, creamed peas, and tapioca pudding. She always enjoyed hearing Charles's prayer of gratitude. It helped to remind her that life at times can be good—it just didn't seem that way now. The food before her was food old people ate. Food served to her in the hospital. Food her grandma ate during her final days. Soft, easy-to-chew, easy-to-swallow food. Boring food.

Slurping, smacking, a slight belch from Mom, a hiccup of indigestion from Charles, a swish of water from Nicole, and what did she think that was? Mouthwash? A squeal of giggles from Christopher as he stacked his meatballs on top of one another, then watched as they tumbled down his small mountain of spaghetti.

The pudding. She would start on the pudding. She took a spoonful and held it in her mouth before swallowing to savor the cool sweetness.

Christopher rolled his meatballs around the edge of the plate with his finger. "Zoe," he said, "how come you kept asking for Grandma when you were in the hospital?"

She wasn't too certain that he wasn't more interested in his meatballs than he was her answer. But she didn't have an answer.

"I don't remember asking for Grandma," she said.

But as soon as she spoke those words, something felt wrong. Like she should remember. A gap, a void, a dark hole seemed to lodge in her memory, her synapses misfired, backfired, something, and she couldn't seem to shake the fog loose and find that memory.

"You kept talking about how she said you couldn't stay," Nicole said, spaghetti dangling from her mouth. "You were saying all kinds of weird things."

Asking for Grandma. The memory. What was it? If there even was one.

Christopher pushed his index fingers into his meatballs. "You wanted to go home, but I said you had to get all better first. Remember?"

"Ah, no, I don't remember," she said, lightly tapping her fork against her plate. "But I do remember something. Something about Grandma."

"Grandma's in heaven," Christopher said.

"Grandma's in heaven," she said slowly. "That's it! I remember now. I was with her."

"Zoe?" her mom said, wiping sauce from her mouth. "Are you okay?"

Zoe stopped tapping her fork and looked up at her

mom. "Grandma and I went into this huge crystal palace and there were scrolls, so many scrolls, and there were fairies and these singers and they glowed in so many beautiful colors and—"

"That's quite the dream," Charles said.

"It wasn't a dream."

"Zoe, those hospital drugs can really mess up a person," Charles said, patting her hand.

Zoe took her hand away. "No, Charles, I think I had one of those things. One of those experiences, like dying, but not dying."

"Pass the parmesan, Nicole," Mom said.

"You think you died?" Nicole asked, passing the parmesan to her mom.

Her mom spooned the cheese onto her pasta. "Zoe, you were in bad shape," she said. "It was just a dream. Now come on, eat."

"You don't believe me?"

"I believe you," Christopher said, holding his index fingers in the air, meatballs attached.

"Christopher, stop playing with your food and eat," Mom said. "And use your silverware, please."

"I read where it can take up to three weeks, maybe longer, for hospital drugs to get out of your system," Nicole said. "You'll probably be spacey for awhile. I mean like really spacey."

"You need to rest and take it easy," Charles said. "But whatever we can do to make it easier, just let us know."

And was that all it was? A dream? The drugs? How could

it have been? It seemed so real. Zoe stared at her plate for a moment, then dipped her spoon into her pudding and swirled it around and around and around. How could it not have been real? It had to be real. Didn't it? Maybe it didn't matter. She decided that it didn't matter.

She glanced up at Charles. Maybe now. Maybe now she should pass the letter to him. He seemed so soft, so relaxed, so kind. Her stepfather usually was kind. He rarely lost his cool. He said that if you're going to argue, argue intelligently. She didn't quite understand how one could argue intelligently, but maybe when she got older she'd understand. He was so different from her biological father, and she often wondered how it was possible that her mom could have married two guys so different from one another.

She decided she would wait. She didn't want to do this in front of The Innocent or Little Miss Perfect.

Charles tossed his napkin onto his plate. "Another great dinner, my dear. Now, what's for dessert?"

Mom picked up her plate and Christopher's. "Blueberry pie will be served after Nicole and Christopher help me clean up."

"Zoe helping too?" Christopher asked with a pout.

"Zoe needs to speak with your dad."

Christopher slumped in his chair and crossed his arms.

"Come on, Christopher," Nicole said. "You want some blueberry pie, don't you?"

He perked up and nodded excitedly.

"The sooner we help Mom, the sooner you'll get pie," she said.

He jumped out of his chair and ran into the kitchen with Nicole running after him, tickling his sides. When the sound of Christopher's giggles faded, Zoe knew it was time. She reached into her pocket, pulled out the letter, and slid it over to Charles.

"What's this?" he asked, pulling his reading glasses from his shirt pocket.

Zoe let out a long yawn, said she was tired and going off to bed. She hadn't gotten but a few feet when Charles let out a heavy sigh.

"Young lady?"

Zoe stopped and turned around.

"Am I going with you, or is your mom?"

That's it? That's all he has to say?

"Mom can go with me."

"All right then. Let me know how it goes." He stood up, handed her the letter, and gently hugged her. "I'll be praying for you."

He always reminded her that if you pray, why worry? If you're worried after prayer, then where's your faith?

Zoe hadn't mastered that praying thing yet. It wasn't something they were raised on. They never went to church, and nobody in the town cared whether they did or not. The town was too big for anyone to care.

Charles had told her how there was no need to enter into a church, a place of walls, because God's church was found in Nature, in the woods, in the fresh air, in the streams and in the rivers, in rocks, and in flowers. God and Nature. Nature and God. And that's how Zoe had felt when she had visited her grandma, that God and Nature were surrounding her and embracing her. She wondered if she'd ever feel that way again. Maybe it was just a dream, but she knew she had felt something—something magnificent, something wonderful, something inexplicable. It was something. Wasn't it?

Chapter Eight

Zoe stood in her bedroom, looking into the mirror. Her scar had transformed from purple to pink and her eyebrow was growing back. She wore the cervical collar only when she felt neck fatigue, and she used the cane only when walking long distances. Every day she felt more victorious, like a warrior. And today she really needed to feel like one.

She debated whether or not to play a game of manipulation with the judge. She looked at her reflection, holding her cane in one hand, her collar in the other. Should she wear the collar and walk into the courtroom with the cane? Would that evoke sympathy from the judge, enough that he would throw her case out? Would she look vulnerable, or merely pathetic?

She tossed both the cane and the collar onto her bed.

Turning back to the mirror, she ran her fingers through her hair. The night before, her mom had helped her remove her purple highlights and lighten her hair. Zoe liked her new look, more than she thought she would. She knew this was a time that commanded change, and her mom seemed overly eager to oblige.

She threw open her closet doors and rummaged through her clothes. Vintage and gothic clothing, worn and torn jeans, sweats, hoodies, T-shirts, and grays and blacks, and more grays and blacks. She felt a tinge of panic. Nothing in this closet was going to make a good impression on the judge. Maybe she'd need to play the sympathy card after all. She glanced at the cane and the collar, let out a heavy sigh, closed her closet doors, then headed down the hall to her sister's room.

She lightly knocked. "Hey, Nicole, sorry to interrupt, but I'm going to—"

"Oh my god," Nicole said, looking up from her laptop. "What did you do to your hair?"

"Do you like it?" Zoe asked.

"Like it? I love it. I never thought of you as a strawberry blond, but it works. It really makes your blue eyes stand out."

"Thanks, Nicole. Well, anyway, I'm going to court this morning and I was wondering if I could look through your closet and pick something out."

"Yeah, sure, go ahead."

She stepped into Nicole's closet. She saw a hunter-green shirt and thought it might look good with her new hair color. She looked it over carefully before placing it back on the rod. She saw a navy-and-white-striped shirt. Cute, but not quite right. She saw a white linen blouse. Pretty, but still not right. Then she saw it. In the back of the closet. The perfect top.

She emerged from the closet. "Can I borrow this one?"

Nicole looked up, and Zoe thought she detected a look of shock, layered in disbelief, in her sister's eyes.

"You don't want me to borrow this one?" Zoe asked.

"No, I mean yes, you can borrow that one," Nicole said. "But I thought you hated pink."

"Well, today, I love pink," Zoe said, smiling.

***

Zoe stood in front of the judge, the same judge as before, only this time he wasn't headless. She thought back to that day and wondered how she could have been so brazen as to show up to court stoned.

While she did feel good in her sister's pink top and her new hairstyle, she didn't feel as confident as she had hoped. Her legs felt wobbly, like when she had first crawled out of that hospital bed and fallen into the arms of the nurse.

"Ms. Zoe Weber."

She stood up straight and looked him in the eye. "Yes, sir."

He held the bow of his eyeglasses between his thumb and forefinger, dangling them as he spoke. "I believe you've been in my courtroom before."

"Yes, sir, I have."

"I almost didn't recognize you, young lady."

Am I supposed to say thank you? Something? Anything? Okay, maybe nothing. I'll just say nothing.

He put on his glasses.

A shiver went up her spine.

"Zoe Weber," the judge said, "you've been brought here today to answer to charges of possession of drugs and drug paraphernalia. Do you understand the charges?"

"I do," Zoe replied.

"Do you understand your rights?"

"I do."

"How do you plead?"

How do I plead? Crazy? Insane? I think I died that morning.

Her mom gently nudged her and whispered to her to answer the question.

Zoe looked up at the judge. "Guilty, Your Honor."

His eyes softened. "Are you pleading guilty voluntarily?" he asked.

"Yes."

"And your mom agrees with the plea?"

"I do," her mom said, softly.

The judge asked Zoe if she had anything she wanted to say. A million thoughts ran through her mind, but she said no. And that was it. And like last time, the judge ordered her to pay a fine, but unlike last time, he also ordered her to perform community service.

She breathed a sigh of relief. She felt the tears rushing up, but she couldn't, she wouldn't. Not here. Not now. Not in front of the judge. Not in front of all these other kids and their parents waiting to speak of their own problems. How embarrassing would that be?

She waited until she felt safe in her mom's SUV before allowing the tears to fall, and she wept not only for what had just happened, but also for all the hurt and pain that had gone before, and she wondered why this thing called life had to hurt so damn much.

Chapter Nine

Zoe rested in Charles's recliner, and while she felt somewhat guilty claiming it from him, she remembered what he had said: "Whatever we can do to make things easier, just let us know." So, she let him know. Charles didn't seem to mind.

She knew she should be calling around to ask about community service. Instead, she worked on her drawing of her princess warrior, shading in the breastplate, concentrating on getting the reflection of light off the metal just right.

The doorbell chimed.

She ignored it. But then she wondered, *Could it be Dylan?* She hadn't heard from him since the accident. If so, now was the perfect time. Mom was at the shop, Charles was on his mail route, Nicole was at college, and Christopher was at the park with the babysitter.

What would Dylan say? What would he do? Would he hug her, kiss her, tell her he was sorry? Would he say, "Let's go get stoned"? She wasn't so sure she'd even want to. Things seemed so different now.

And what would she say?

"Lucky you. A few scratches."

Maybe this love thing wasn't worth it.

The doorbell sounded again.

She hoped it wasn't him. Then she hoped it was. But whoever it was, they weren't going away. She grabbed her cane and peered out the bay window. Aunt Maggie's Lexus SUV was parked out front, and Aunt Maggie stood on the front stoop, Starbucks coffee in one hand, cell phone in the other.

Zoe opened the door.

"Good morning, Zoe," Aunt Maggie said before hitting a button on her cell phone, then tossing it into her oversized black leather bag. "Sorry to barge in so early in the morning."

"It's ten thirty," said Zoe.

Maggie waved her hand. "Your mom called, which gave me this really great idea. I only have a few minutes. Can we talk?" Maggie rushed in and plopped down on the sofa.

The coffee buzz had definitely kicked in.

"How would you like to do your community service at the hospital with me?" Maggie asked.

Zoe sat on the arm of the recliner, resting her hands on the top of her cane, and just as she was about to respond, her aunt continued, "Look, I get it. The whole community service thing. Oh, hell, I was doing the same stuff when I was your age."

And before Zoe could fully process that statement, or confession, or whatever that was, her aunt said, "So, what do you think?"

"You work with people who are dying," Zoe said, slowly contemplating her aunt's crazy idea.

"Well, some are, some aren't," Maggie said. She took a big gulp of her coffee. "It's all good."

Zoe wondered if it wasn't more than just coffee in that mug.

Maggie continued, "I wouldn't have ended up in the medical field had it not been for my community service." She jingled her car keys. "I need to get to work, but think about it."

Maggie got up to leave, but the sketch pad caught her attention. She stared at the drawing. "Zoe, this is impressive. I always knew you had talent, but you've really improved since the last time I saw your work at your school's spring art show."

Maggie stared at the drawing for what Zoe thought was an unusually long time.

"This is really good," her aunt said, emphasizing each word.

"You think so?"

Maggie nodded. "Definitely much more feeling in this piece, more detail, and such emotion in her dark eyes. She's dangerous, strong looking, yet vulnerable. I really feel drawn in." Maggie chuckled. "No pun intended."

No pun intended. Why does that sound so familiar?

Maggie gave her keys one last jingle before heading out the door.

Zoe looked at her princess warrior. She did look dangerous, strong, and vulnerable. Vulnerable. That's how Zoe was beginning to feel at the thought of going back into the hospital. Mixed emotions played in her psyche. She brushed the thoughts away, plopped back down in the recliner, and continued sketching the breastplate, a most necessary piece of armor in battle. And why did she suddenly feel as though she was about to face a battle of her own, one of the biggest battles of her life?

***

Zoe stepped into the elevator of St. Francis Hospital, the same hospital that she'd recovered in from her accident. The same hospital she'd been born in. The same hospital her grandma had died in. Lung cancer. And she hadn't smoked a cigarette a day in her life. So sudden, so fast. A life so strong, yet so delicate.

She pushed button three, which would take her to Aunt Maggie's floor. She couldn't believe that she was actually going through with her aunt's plan.

She stepped off the elevator, steadying herself with her cane. She looked down the cold, sterile corridor. Maggie's office was at the far end. How was it that it had never seemed so far before? She passed the nurses station. Two nurses talked softly to one another, while another nurse swiped an eraser across a white board, erasing a patient's name and room number. Zoe hoped that was a good thing.

Still looking at the white board, lost in her thoughts, someone suddenly slammed into her. Her body swayed, her knees buckled, and her cane slipped from her hand and hit the tile floor with a *cling-a-ting-ting*.

"I gotcha," the man said, grabbing her. He held her steady. "You okay?"

"Yeah, I think so."

"Sorry about that," he said, reaching for her cane.

His sandy blond hair hung over his forehead, touching the rimless glasses that adorned his hazel eyes. A stethoscope hung around his neck, and a pocket protector holding way too many pens bulged from the pocket of his lab coat.

He handed her the cane. "Do you need help finding someone?"

"I'm here to see my aunt Maggie," she said, taking the cane, "but I know where her office is."

Zoe thought she detected a look of surprise in his eyes before he said, "And you're sure you're okay?"

She nodded.

"Well, then, have a good day."

"Thanks. You too."

He sure was a nice guy, Zoe thought, *although someone needs to tell doctors that pocket protectors don't look cool.* Then she wondered if those stethoscopes were sanitized after each use.

Zoe peeked into Maggie's office. Her aunt sat behind a large oak desk in a white leather chair, keying away at her laptop. Framed awards, certificates, and licenses hung on the wall. Margaret Ellis, PhD, RN Psychology, Certified Grief Therapist, Certified Clinical Nurse Specialist.

Maggie looked up. "Good morning, Zoe. Come on in."

"Good morning, Aunt Maggie."

"I'm so glad you've decided to do this," she said.

"Me too," Zoe said.

A lie.

Did Zoe dare tell her that it wasn't her decision? Her mom had come home that morning to grab her bank deposit bag and saw Maggie drive away, and after Zoe told her mom the reason for the visit, her mom made the decision for her. Her mom thought it was a great idea.

Zoe continued, "But I'm a little nervous."

The truth.

"Zoe, you're going to be fine. And look at you," Maggie said, coming around the desk to take Zoe's hands in hers. "I can't believe how much better you look in only a few days."

"If only I could get rid of this cane," Zoe said. "But I guess I'll fit right in with everyone else here."

Maggie grinned. "Yes, pretty much canes and wheelchairs on this floor." She picked up a folder from off her desk and flipped through it. "I think I'll start you off with Matt."

"Matt?"

"I do have to warn you, though. He's a bit of a grouch."

"My first day here and you're sticking me with a grouchy old man?"

Maggie laughed, and Zoe thought she detected a mischievous twinkle in her eyes. "His room is on the other end of the corridor," she said, putting the folder back down. "Last room on the left."

"You're not coming with me?"

She shook her head.

Knowing she'd been defeated, Zoe walked back down the corridor, past the elevators, and down to the other end. She decided that if nothing else, she was certainly getting her exercise.

She lightly tapped on the door.

A guy in a wheelchair was staring out the window.

"Matt?"

No response.

"Matt?"

She walked into the room.

"Hi, I'm Zoe," she said loudly.

She stepped to his side. Then, she stepped in front of him.

"You're blocking my view," he said flatly.

She moved out of his way and looked out the window.

A brick wall? He's staring at a brick wall across the courtyard.

Maggie was right. He was a grouch, and he probably had that stupid grouchy attitude long before he got sick, which is probably why he got sick. Maggie had lied. She wasn't going to be fine. Her mom had lied. This was not a good idea. This was a mistake, a waste of her time. She felt like marching right on out of there to Maggie's office to tell her how stupid this whole thing was. She'd never be good at this anyway. And why would anyone ever think differently?

She wanted to tell Matt to wait while she found someone else to take him on his stroll, but something compelled her to stay, and so she stood there looking at him, and in those brief moments, she realized that he wasn't much older than her. Late teens, maybe early twenties. She felt like she should feel sorry for him, yet she didn't.

She leaned her cane against the wall. "Do you need to take anything?"

Matt continued to stare out the window.

"Okay," she said. "I'll take that as a no."

She grabbed the handles of his wheelchair and started to push him away from the window, but the wheelchair wouldn't budge.

"You have to release the brake," he said.

"How do you do that?"

Without answering, he reached down and abruptly jerked a lever.

Zoe felt like taking that lever and putting it somewhere.

"Well, are we going now," he said, "or like most women, did you change your mind?"

"Going already," Zoe said.

She grabbed hold of the wheelchair and wheeled Matt out of his room, down the corridor, and into the elevator. The longest elevator ride ever. Once outside, she looked around, trying to figure out where to park his butt.

"So, any steep hills around here?" she mumbled under her breath.

"What did you say?"

"Oh, aaah, cheap thrills! I asked if there were any cheap thrills around here."

"What's your name again?"

"Zoe."

"Zoe, there aren't any cheap thrills around here. There

aren't any expensive thrills around here. There aren't any thrills around here, period. Just get me to that tree over there and stop talking so much."

"Yes, sir."

She wheeled Matt under the broad branches of a massive oak tree and plopped down a few feet from him. She pulled out her iPod and put in her ear buds. After about fifteen minutes, he waved his hand toward the hospital doors.

She wheeled him back into the hospital, rode the slowest elevator ride again, then wheeled him into his room and to the window with that view. She set the brake and, without saying good-bye, left, hoping she'd never have to set that brake again. She thought about her grandma's hospice nurse and how wrong she was. It wasn't only the nice people who got cancer.

She walked to Maggie's office with the intention of telling her she was done. Not only with Matt, but with the whole thing, but as soon as she stepped into Maggie's office, her aunt jumped up from behind her desk and clapped her hands in glee.

My god, she's worse than a little kid at Christmas.

"I have another wonderful patient for you to visit," Maggie said.

Who was the first one?

"I've told her all about you, and she's so excited to meet you. Her name is Grace Martin. Come with me."

Before Zoe could convince her aunt otherwise, she found herself walking down the corridor alongside her.

"Well, here we are," she said, pointing to the room.

Sunlight streamed in through a large window, the warm rays casting a golden hue across the room, and the room seemed to breathe in the glow of the light. She looked at the small, frail woman sitting up in bed. Her eyes were gray and wet. Zoe wondered if she'd been crying.

"How are you feeling today, Grace?" Maggie asked.

"Hello, Dr. Ellis. I'm doing all right." She looked past Maggie. "Is this the young lady you were telling me about?"

"She is, and she's going to keep you company today."

"That's wonderful."

"Sorry to cut this short, but I need to get back to my office," Maggie said. "If you need anything, Zoe, you know where to find me."

Maggie left before Zoe had any time to protest. She didn't want Maggie to leave. She didn't want to be left alone with a woman who looked like she could die at any moment. She wanted to confess that this wasn't her idea, but she then glanced at Mrs. Martin, who was looking at her, and she thought she saw a glimmer of appreciation in her eyes, and a look of hopeful anticipation.

"Well, don't I feel special having such a sweet young lady to visit with me," Grace said.

"Thank you, Mrs. Martin. I'm glad to be here," Zoe said. She wondered if God forgave all lies.

"Call me Grace, dear, and make yourself comfortable," she said, pointing her arthritic finger toward a blue swivel rocker. "If you were in my home, I'd offer you some tea. Tea with honey and freshly squeezed lemon. Wouldn't that be grand? But I'm not home, and I'm not so sure I ever will be."

Zoe pushed a green afghan out of her way before sitting down.

"Oh, here, honey, let me take that."

She handed the afghan to Mrs. Martin, then leaned back in the chair and gently rocked. The chair felt almost as comfortable as Charles's recliner. Almost.

"Your aunt tells me you're an artist, and a very good one."

"Ah, yeah, I guess so," Zoe said.

Mrs. Martin looked at her expectantly.

Zoe continued, "I work in pencil and watercolor."

"Sounds lovely," Mrs. Martin said.

Silence. Now what. Feeling awkward. . .

Mrs. Martin coughed a raspy cough. She reached for a tissue and dabbed her mouth. "If you wouldn't mind, you could read to me. My eyes aren't what they used to be." She pointed to a book sitting on top of a dresser.

Zoe felt relieved. Reading would be much better than any superficial small talk. She most certainly didn't want to talk to her about her life. What could Mrs. Martin possibly understand about her friends, school, Dylan, partying?

Zoe picked up the book and caught a whiff of the red roses with baby's breath sitting atop the dresser, roses that smelled as wonderful and lovely as the flowers in her mom's shop. She sat back down and took a good look at the book. A slight groan escaped from her. She remembered this novel, *The Scarlet Letter*, from freshman lit. Now here it was again, like a persistent ghost.

"It's on my bucket list," Mrs. Martin said, softly.

"Excuse me?"

"I was supposed to read it in high school, but I was too busy chasing boys."

Zoe burst out laughing, but quickly covered her mouth.

Mrs. Martin chuckled. "It's okay, dear. I know, hard to believe I ever used to chase boys, but I did, and I caught one. Harvey was his name. We were married right out of high school. We had a daughter. Worked on the farm. Milked cows. Rode horses. Gardened. Good country living before moving to the city to be closer to my daughter and her husband and the grandkids. Harvey died about ten years ago. The old ticker gave out." She looked at Zoe with misty eyes. "Go ahead, dear."

Zoe began reading and soon realized that the story was as awful as she had remembered. She read a few more pages before she heard soft snoring. She looked at Mrs. Martin, her grayish lips puttering with every exhale.

She laid the book back on the dresser, gently placed the afghan over Mrs. Martin, and sat with her, watching her chest rise and fall ever so slightly. She looked so peaceful. Zoe wondered where her dreams took her. Did they take her to Harvey and walks through the countryside with him? Did they take her to a place where she could run through wide-open fields, ride her horses, be with her cows, and watch as spring brought new life to the farm? When a person was close to death, did their dreams feel more real to them than their memories?

She shifted in the chair. It felt very comfortable. Too comfortable.

Her own dream took her to a meadow filled with

wildflowers and lavender and to her grandma, and together they walked hand in hand, but when she looked away and then back again, it was Mrs. Martin's hand in hers.

They ran through the meadow and came upon a pond with a pier. They ran down the pier, and just when they were about to jump into the water, Zoe awoke. She sat still for a few moments, feeling the worn fabric of the rocker under her fingers. The sound of snoring brought her fully awake. She stood and tucked the afghan tighter around Mrs. Martin, and as she did so, she wondered why her hands felt tingly, as though they were still asleep. She shook them, then held them still. A few moments later, the tingling stopped.

Memories quietly slipped in of her grandmother in hospice. Her grandmother was as sick then as Mrs. Martin seemed to be now. Zoe knew it would only be a matter of time before Mrs. Martin did indeed see her Harvey again.

Maybe next time I see you, Zoe thought, *I'll tell you all about a place where Harvey just might be, and after I tell you all about it, you won't want to wait to get there.*

Chapter Ten

The more time Zoe spent at the hospital with the patients, the more she grew to appreciate them, and the
profession her aunt had chosen, and the profession her
sister would be entering after graduation in two years. She
also thought how her mom and her aunt had been right after all. Once again. This was not as depressing and scary as
she had thought it would be. But still, she knew this medical
stuff wasn't for her.

She walked into Mrs. Martin's room and, after a quick
hello, grabbed the book from off the top of the dresser. She
hooked her cane over the arm of the blue swivel rocker,
made herself comfortable, and opened *The Scarlet Letter*
to chapter 3, "The Recognition," the part where the creepy,
thought-to-be-dead husband recognized his wife standing
on the scaffold with child in arms, and where the Reverend
Mr. Dimmesdale demanded Hester reveal the father of her
child. She remembered how Hester couldn't, wouldn't reveal the father, telling everyone that her child would never
know an earthly father, only a Father in heaven.

It's not like she'd lied or anything. She just wouldn't reveal the truth, and sometimes the truth has to be concealed in order to get through this thing called life. Right? It's called protecting. Isn't it?

Zoe glanced up at Mrs. Martin.

Mrs. Martin smiled at her. And in that smile, something seemed different to Zoe. It was something in Mrs. Martin's eyes. They seemed bluer than gray today, and her skin tone seemed more pink than ashen. She wore pink pajamas with a matching robe lined in rose satin trim, and Zoe thought she looked quite pretty, almost youthful as she sat up in bed waiting for her to begin reading. Her expression was one of childlike anticipation, and Zoe almost giggled, her smile was so big.

Perhaps they'd changed her medication, or perhaps her daughter and grandkids were visiting more often. Or maybe it was the way the sunlight was filtering in and reflecting the pink of her pajamas onto her face.

Before Zoe began to read, she brushed her fingertips across the words on the purple bookmark: *Trust in the Lord with all thine heart, and lean not unto thine own understanding; In all thy ways acknowledge him, and he shall direct thy paths.*

"Mrs. Martin?"

"Yes, Zoe."

"Do you believe what it says here on this bookmark? About trusting in the Lord?"

The look on Mrs. Martin's face gave her the answer. It was as if the Lord himself moved right through her. Her eyes lit up and she smiled, and in that smile, the years seemed to roll off her frail body, leaving a luminescent quality radiating in, through, and around her.

"Yes, I do believe, Zoe."

"And this part about 'lean not unto thine own understanding'?"

"I do."

"So when bad things happen, it's not okay to ask why? You mean we just have to live with it?"

Mrs. Martin pointed to Zoe's forehead and then to her cane in one graceful sweep. "You had what you would probably call an accident?"

Zoe nodded. "Yes, it was an accident. A car accident."

Mrs. Martin leaned toward her. "You see, my dear, there are no such things as accidents. To say there are accidents is to say we live in a chaotic world, which is to say that God must not know what He's doing. I believe God does know what He's doing. It just doesn't appear that way to us. We're so limited by our senses that it's difficult for us to understand the Truth of what's really happening."

"My car accident wasn't an accident?"

"Everything is unfolding exactly as it should," she said, "and in time you'll see that. Patience, my dear. Patience."

"Everything?"

"Well, I think the universe does hiccup once in a while, but not often," she said with a wink.

Should Zoe tell her? Should she tell her about the accident, which according to Mrs. Martin, wasn't an accident. Should she tell her how wonderful it was to leave the body and go to heaven? And that when in heaven, she will be able to read all the books in the world, all the books ever written, and her eyes will never grow tired? Should she tell her of the magnificent beauty, the kind of beauty that makes you want to fall to your knees and weep?

Mrs. Martin grew silent, leaned back, and closed her eyes.

Perhaps another time.

Zoe placed the afghan over Mrs. Martin, quietly sat back down, and continued to read *The Scarlet Letter*. She decided that she actually liked Hester Prynne. She liked her spirit, her steadfast resolution to hold true to her convictions, her devotion to her child. It certainly wasn't a story that she would have ever put on her bucket list, but she was glad now that it was on Mrs. Martin's, even though she might not live long enough to hear it through to the end.

She finished chapter 3, then realized that she was late for Matt's stroll. She grabbed her cane, put the book back on top of the dresser, and made her way to Grump's room.

"Hey, Zoe, how's it going?" he asked, looking up at her with a smile.

She was taken aback by his expression. He hadn't smiled since she'd met him. Was he up to something? Planning something? But it wasn't a devious smile, more like an "I'm actually glad you're here" smile.

She grabbed the green-and-blue plaid flannel blanket from off his bed. "We might need this," she said, placing it on Matt's lap. "It's supposed to get cool this afternoon."

She wheeled him outside to the oak tree, spread out

the blanket, and helped him from his wheelchair, and as she did, his agility surprised her. He seemed to move with greater ease and litheness than before, and his movements seemed to correspond with his attitude. Maybe the sunshine was doing him some good.

They looked up between the branches at the cloudless sky. The sunlight filtered through, and the shadows and the light danced across their faces. Zoe told Matt about her little brother and how he believed that when the branches sway in the breeze, God is waving and saying hi.

"Smart kid," said Matt.

"I know," said Zoe.

She listened as Matt talked about his parents and his sister and how difficult this was for them. They'd made the trip to Avalon a few times, but living in Chicago, they could only do so much.

"Cubs or Sox?" Zoe asked.

"Cubs, of course!"

"Right on," Zoe said, giving him a high-five even though she didn't care either way.

He told her about his girlfriend, Katrina, but everyone called her Kat. Her name was appropriate, he said, because she moved as gracefully as one. They met in Aspen, on the ski slopes, and had been dating for a little over a year.

"I was going to propose to her," he said.

"Why haven't you?" Zoe asked.

"Upon learning how sick I am, she left." He rubbed his eyes. "She's a good person. She deserves better."

And before Zoe could even offer him any words of

encouragement, the sun and the breeze and the songs of the birds lulled them both to sleep.

The scent of freshly mowed grass.

The warm sun on her face.

A soft hand.

She slowly opened her eyes. Fluffy, white clouds moved peacefully across an azure sky. She slipped her hand from Matt's, sat up, and looked at him. He seemed so deep in his dreams. So still. Or dead.

"Matt? You okay?"

No answer, but Zoe was used to nonanswers from Matt, although not today. She slightly shook him. He mumbled, and she breathed a sigh of relief.

She helped him back into his wheelchair, wheeled him back to his room, helped him into bed, and spread the blanket over him. As soon as his head hit the pillow, he was asleep again. Zoe couldn't help but wonder if perhaps it wasn't a broken heart that was killing him.

Chapter Eleven

Zoe counted down the days to when her fine would be paid off and her mother would actually start paying her for working at the shop, but pay or no pay, she did enjoy creating elaborate window displays to attract shoppers into the store. She enjoyed her little game of manipulation. The shoppers would stop, look, point, and then she would hear the door chime and would grin in satisfaction as the person who had once stood outside now stood inside—buying things.

But today, she didn't care about the shoppers. She didn't care if they admired her artistic knowledge of composition, color, and texture. She worked the window because from this vantage point, she could see the Abyss Bookstore front window and maybe Dylan.

She still hadn't seen or heard from him since the accident. Her mother and Charles forbade her. Her mother told her that he had better not step foot in the shop again, which made Zoe feel sad. She wanted to see him, even if it was only a glimpse from a store window.

She wished that she entered and left the store by the front, as he did. Then maybe they'd be opening and locking up at the same time. They would wave to each other from across the street, then walk into the street and meet in the middle. And talk and laugh and be silly. Just like they used to be.

She tied a purple ribbon around a crystal vase of yellow tulips and occasionally glanced at the bookstore window. Nothing. No movement. She'd be patient. She could work this window all day if she had to.

She heard the door chime and glanced up. A dark-haired, middle-aged woman had entered. Zoe glanced back at the window. Then she saw something. A shadowy figure. She squinted. She thought it was him, but she wasn't sure.

"Excuse me," the woman said. "Miss?"

Zoe turned and looked at her.

"I'm trying to find something for my daughter," the woman said. "She loves angels. Do you have any angel necklaces?"

Zoe was about to point to a glass case by the register, but her mom entered from the storage room and asked the woman if she was finding everything okay.

"I got it, Mom," Zoe said.

"There they are," her mom said, grabbing her reading glasses from off the checkout counter. "Let me know if you need anything." She then retreated to the storage room.

"Right this way," Zoe said, leading the woman to the case. "We have some angel necklaces with birthstones."

"That sounds perfect," the woman said.

The woman scanned the case. Zoe wished she would hurry up. The woman stared at a sterling silver angel necklace, an emerald on the angel's heart.

"Would you like to take a closer look at that one?" Zoe asked.

The woman nodded.

Zoe pulled the necklace from the case and handed it to her.

The woman held it in her hands, almost reverently.

"That's my birthstone," Zoe said. "How old is your daughter?"

"Sixteen."

"That's how old I am," Zoe said. "What school does she go to?"

"She doesn't."

Zoe looked at the woman and into her dark eyes. A tear had formed. Zoe wanted to say something, but didn't know what.

"She's home-schooled," the woman said, staring at the necklace.

"Oh," Zoe said, not sure how to proceed. The air felt heavy, and she felt awkward.

The woman continued, "It's easier for her that way."

Zoe wanted to ask what she meant, but at the same time, she didn't want to be standing here all afternoon helping this woman. She had a window to get back to.

"It's lovely," the woman finally said. "I'll take it."

As soon as the woman left, Zoe headed back to the window. No movement now. She waited. Then waited some more. It didn't take long before she felt pathetic.

She spent the rest of the day ringing up customers,

listening to their stories behind the reason or the occasion for the gift, and wondering why they felt the need to tell her their story. She grew weary of all the stories: stories on divorce, marriage, retirement, a baby, graduation, a veteran's homecoming. Okay, that one didn't annoy her. She congratulated the couple on their happy reunion with their son and wished them all the best.

The day flew by, and just as she was about to lock up, a woman in her early twenties gracefully breezed in. Her long, auburn ponytail swished back and forth through the hole in her baseball cap. Athletic. Toned. Tanned. Pretty.

"Do you sell essential oils?" she asked.

"We do," Zoe said, pointing toward the display of oils and their associated herb or flower.

The woman carefully looked over the oils, then flipped through a book on oils. She sighed heavily.

"Any conditions you want to lessen or alleviate?" Zoe asked.

The woman didn't look up but continued flipping through the book. "Depression," she said.

Zoe grabbed a bottle of chamomile and a bottle of frankincense. "These are great for alleviating depression, stress, anxiety, things like that."

"I'll take them," the woman said.

As they walked to the checkout counter, the young woman said, "I hope they help."

Zoe didn't want to ask, didn't want to know. She wasn't in the mood for another sob story. Between working at the shop and the hospital, she had heard and seen enough.

The woman chuckled. "And to think I used to buy stuff like this for a boyfriend," she said, her feline-like green eyes growing misty. "He never did believe in the healing power of essential oils or any of that alternative holistic stuff. I'm not so sure I do either, but I think it's good to at least try different things. Don't you?"

"Oh, yes, definitely," Zoe said.

She quickly rang up the purchase, thanked the woman, then walked her to the door.

"I'm sorry if I kept you late," the woman said. "Thanks again."

And with that, she left. Zoe locked up, but not before taking one last look out that front window.

Chapter Twelve

Zoe stepped off the elevator and bounced her cane down the corridor with a rhythmic *tap, tap, tap* toward Mrs. Martin's room. She had finished reading chapter 13, "Another View of Hester," and she looked forward to continuing with the story even if Mrs. Martin did fall asleep. She tapped her way into Mrs. Martin's room, but as soon as she stepped inside, froze.

The family pictures were gone. The afghan was gone. The bouquet of red roses, now withered and dark, had been dumped into the trash container by the dresser. And the book, the story that Zoe had grown to cherish reading to Mrs. Martin, was gone. Her stomach tumbled and her throat tightened. She slowly backed out of the room, then quickly walked down the corridor.

"Why didn't you tell me?" she said, rushing into her aunt's office. "Why didn't you tell me Mrs. Martin died?"

Zoe stiffened as her eyes slowly went from her aunt's startled look to two men standing in her office. The tall, dark-haired one stopped writing and looked up from his notepad, and the other one, stocky and bald, stopped abruptly in midsentence and glared at her.

A hundred thoughts flooded in. Who were these men and why were they looking at her as though she had just committed a crime? She wished she could disappear, or better yet, that those two would disappear.

The wheels on Maggie's chair squeaked as she pushed herself away from her desk. "I'll be right back, if you'll please excuse me." She took Zoe by the arm and led her into the corridor.

"Zoe, Mrs. Martin didn't die," Maggie said.

"Then where is she?" Zoe asked, tears forming. "Why is everything in her room gone?"

Maggie smiled, and Zoe felt as though it seemed forced, as if she was happy for Mrs. Martin, and yet nervous about something at the same time.

"Mrs. Martin made an unexpected, not to mention, remarkable, rebound. In this crazy world of medicine, you never know what's going to happen. We like to think we have everything figured out, but when we think we do—"

"I thought she died."

"Would you like to say good-bye to her?"

"She hasn't left yet?"

"She's on the first floor, last office at the end of the hall. She's with her daughter and son-in-law, signing her release papers. But you'll have to hurry."

"Thanks!" she said, grabbing Maggie and giving her a big hug. "Oh, and sorry I interrupted your meeting. Guess I'd better knock next time."

As she hurried to the elevator, she thought she heard Maggie saying something about hopefully there won't be a next time. She didn't know what she meant by that, but right now she didn't care.

The elevator dinged and Zoe stepped in and pushed the button that would take her to the first floor. Could the door close any slower, and once it did close, she counted down the floors and wondered if the elevator could move any slower? She was happy for Mrs. Martin, and yet puzzled about her quick recovery. The elevator dinged again, and she stepped out and looked down the corridor. At the other end, a middle-aged couple was pushing a woman in a wheelchair, a woman who looked like Mrs. Martin.

"Zoe," the woman said, waving, and in that moment, Zoe knew that it was indeed Mrs. Martin, a woman who only weeks earlier had appeared to have been on her deathbed. And here she was, looking younger and vibrant.

Mrs. Martin reached out her hands. "Zoe, honey, I was so hoping I'd see you before I left. They're letting me go home. Isn't that wonderful?"

Zoe wanted to tell her that yes, that was wonderful, but the words got caught in her throat and all she could do was nod.

"I guess Harvey will have to wait a bit longer," Mrs. Martin said with a bright smile and a wink.

A fog had rolled in, clouding Zoe's thoughts. She had so many things she wanted to tell Mrs. Martin, but all she could think to say was, "I guess he will."

"Zoe, I'd like you to meet my daughter, Lisa, and her husband, Tom."

Lisa stepped from behind the wheelchair and extended her hand. "Thank you so much for taking care of my mom when we couldn't be here. We really appreciate it."

"More than you can ever know," Tom said.

Zoe smiled so as not to cry. "You're welcome." Her voice cracked a little, and she hoped no one noticed.

Mrs. Martin wrapped Zoe's hands in her own and gave them a tight squeeze. "Take care, dear."

She watched as Tom and Lisa wheeled Mrs. Martin down the hallway and out the automatic doors. And even though she was happy for Mrs. Martin, why did she suddenly feel like she had lost her best friend? How was it even possible for a woman who was so sick to have recovered? Zoe wondered if perhaps she hadn't been so sick after all.

Then a memory slowly surfaced, something Nicole had said during breakfast one morning while discussing a subject for her thesis with Mom. Something about placing patients in a room with lots of natural light streaming in. Something about the light helping patients heal and recover much more quickly than patients placed in rooms with little to no natural light. Maybe natural light does make a difference. But could Mrs. Martin's recovery have been that simple?

But something else nagged her. Mrs. Martin's daughter. Zoe knew her from somewhere, but where?

She brushed the thoughts away and got back on the elevator. Matt would be waiting for her. She looked forward to visiting with him, and as usual, she would wheel him outside under the tree where they would talk about stuff.

She realized she was doing most of the talking now and she knew he was supposed to do most of the talking, but he was such a good listener. How could she not talk?

She figured Matt would die anyway, so what did it matter what she revealed to him? She had told him about Dylan, the accident, and her mom and Charles not wanting her to see him, and Matt told her to not let anyone dissuade her from being with someone she loved if that's what she wanted, even though at sixteen what could she possibly know about love?

"It's not a knowing," she had told him. "It's a feeling."

She lightly tapped on his door.

Matt glanced up as he wheeled himself to the dresser. "Hey, Zoe, how's it going?" But before she could answer, he continued, "I have some great news."

He pulled a pile of clothes from the dresser drawer, wheeled back to his bed, and stuffed them into a duffel bag.

"News?" she asked

Matt rested his hand on the bag and looked up at her. "You know I've had tests done almost every week since I've been in here. Well, guess what? All of my tests have come back normal. Normal! I'm well enough to go home! Can you believe it? Crazy, I know, but if anything goes wacky again . . ."

What about their talks, their strolls? *He can't be better,* she thought, even though yes, she wanted him to be better. But her life, her entire life she had poured out to him because she thought he was actually going to die and now he was not and now he knew all of her secrets. If she'd known that he wasn't going to die, she wouldn't have told him any of it. She thought she was going to be ill.

"Zoe, you okay?" he asked.

"No, I mean yes. Yes, that's great you're better," she said. "How cool is that? Totally unexpected, but cool."

He's better. Whoopee! She should feel like dancing! But, she didn't. She wanted to bury her face in embarrassment and never, ever spill her guts to any guy ever again.

"I know we got off to a bad start. I wasn't dealing with life because I wasn't dealing with the thought of dying." He looked up at her. "I want you to know that I'm glad you were relentless in doing your job even when I was being an ass. I appreciate you being with me, and letting me be me, and allowing me to have my temper tantrums. You don't give up on people." He stuffed a shirt into his bag. "Unlike my girlfriend."

He wheeled back to the dresser and reached for a framed photograph.

"Is that her?" Zoe asked.

Matt nodded. "She tried to make things better for me, but I wasn't into all that weird alternative healing stuff like she was." He sighed heavily. "I probably would have left me too."

Zoe looked at the couple in their ski outfits, snow-capped mountains in the distance. They seemed so perfect together. So happy. So healthy. So enchanted with one another. She thought the woman looked pretty, with her long hair and sparkling green eyes.

Matt looked up at Zoe. "This was taken last January.

Hard to believe that I could have gone downhill so fast." He chuckled. "And I'm not talking about skiing, either."

He continued to hold the picture as though it were something sacred. A reverent silence hung in the air, and Zoe breathed it in—the silence felt okay. She wished she could wave a magic wand and transport Matt back to that happier, healthier time and back to those slopes with his girlfriend when going downhill fast still meant skiing.

"I'm sorry things didn't work out," she said, "but maybe now that you're better—"

"I doubt it, but thanks, Zoe," he said. "Thanks for everything."

"I'm going to miss you."

"And I'm going to miss you."

"Oh, I almost forgot." She pulled a Cubs baseball cap from her tote, tugged on the bill, and handed it to him.

He took it in his hands, chuckled, then looked up at her and smiled.

"It wasn't meant to be a going-away present," she said, "because I didn't know you were." She paused. "I hope you like it."

"Like it? I love it. Thanks."

"Do you need any help out?" she asked, feeling the sting of tears forming.

"Zoe, I'd love to have you wheel me out those hospital doors one last time."

He put on the cap. "How do I look?" he asked, grinning.

"Happy," she said, smiling. "Very happy."

And as she wheeled him toward the elevator, she wiped away that tear and wished with all her heart that she'd never, ever said anything about steep hills.

Chapter Thirteen

Zoe thought her aunt had sounded worried when she called. Maybe someone had filed a complaint against her. Maybe she was about to be fired. But was that even possible? To be fired? From community service? As she stepped off the elevator, two men stepped into an elevator directly across from her, the same two men she had seen in Maggie's office. She wondered who they were exactly and what they were doing here. She'd have to ask Maggie after their talk.

She knocked on Maggie's door before realizing she was on the phone. Maggie waved her in and motioned for her to have a seat. Zoe sat down in the chair opposite her desk. Maggie shifted the phone receiver to her other ear, and Zoe waited, feeling awkward, like maybe she should have waited outside until this phone conversation was over.

She picked up a medical journal from the desk and flipped through its glossy pages of medical equipment, bald headed children, some smiling, some not, an article on art, drugs, drugs, and more drugs, an article on skin cancer diagnosis and treatment. Zoe wondered where the article was on cancer prevention.

Maggie said, "Okay, Scott," for what seemed like a hundred times, and Zoe wondered if Scott was the guy who had the final authority to fire her. Maggie hung up the phone, and Zoe shifted in her seat, anticipating a "you're fired" sermon.

Zoe put the journal back on Maggie's desk. "I can do my community service elsewhere if you're not happy with me," she said.

"Zoe, I love having you here, everyone does," Maggie said. "But I'd like to reassign you to another department."

Zoe felt the air being sucked right out of her. Another department? Why?

Maggie continued, "There's a situation here in oncology, and until things have quieted, I'd like for you to participate in the hospital's art program."

A situation and an art program? Zoe wasn't sure which one she wanted to ask Maggie about first. She didn't have to.

Maggie continued, "Hospitals across the nation have implemented art programs with great success, and so we decided to start one here a few months ago. Even Florence Nightingale appreciated the curative influence of beautiful objects." Maggie stood up and walked over to a picture hanging on the wall. "Florence Nightingale," she said, pointing to the picture of a woman wearing a white-lace cap and dark dress with white-lace collar. "We all need our heroes, and she's mine."

Zoe stood up and looked at the picture. "How old was she?"

"In that picture, midthirties."

"Women sure looked old back then."

Maggie laughed. "She was your age when she heard the calling. How many kids your age have such a strong conviction about anything?"

Zoe shrugged. "I have convictions."

Maggie grinned. "She believed that we are affected by form, by color and light in a positive, generating, self-healing way," she said, sitting back down. "Art is a great way to take one's mind off of one's troubles and focus on creating something beautiful. Creative expression has been shown to help reduce stress in patients, and help some gain control over their helplessness, which helps improve mood and reduce anxiety, which improves one's quality of sleep, which improves the immune system."

"It does all that?" Zoe asked.

Maggie nodded and continued to explain the workshops to her and how she would assist the art director in helping the patients express their feelings about their illness through art.

Zoe playfully scolded her aunt for not telling her about this program sooner. She decided that she just might have found where she belonged in this crazy world of medicine. For now, anyway, and in her enthusiasm, she forgot to ask Maggie about that "situation."

***

Zoe tapped on the door to the art director's office. A man of small stature, wearing khakis and a blue gingham shirt, was pulling color photos from off a printer. He turned around.

"Mr. Martinez?" she asked, surprised.

"Zoe? Well, isn't this a pleasant surprise," Mr. Martinez said. "Dr. Ellis told me that I would be training someone, but I didn't realize it would be you." He walked over and extended his hand to her in a warm handshake. "Welcome to the art therapy program."

"You actually work here?"

"I'm a volunteer," he said, "and I love it. Gives me a nice break from teaching art at Rock Ridge. This is relatively less stressful."

Zoe chuckled. "Yeah, I think I get that teacher-student stress thing."

He smiled. "And you, Ms. Zoe Weber, are going to do fine. I know your work, and it's impressive."

"Thanks."

And so the training began, and Mr. Martinez trained her on what to say and on how to say it. He taught her how to be an effective observer and listener, not a critic, not a judge, but to support whatever choices the kids make. And after a few days, Mr. Martinez knew Zoe was ready. She wasn't so sure.

"And remember, Zoe, in the art therapy room, they are artists, not patients," he said.

"Got it," she said.

"And I'm here for you if you need me," he said.

She thanked him, then walked into the art room. About fifteen kids sat at tables, either painting or drawing. Some of the kids looked very sick, and others didn't appear as though anything was wrong. Some had hair, some didn't. Some were quite thin, others not so much.

They are not patients, Zoe silently reminded herself.

Artists, they are artists.

She walked around the room, between the tables. A boy about thirteen had painted a tree with big red birds perched on stiff and twisted black branches. The painting looked like globs of blood dripping from an arthritic, lifeless form.

Is that how that boy feels? Like the life force is slowly dripping out of him, like a dying tree, its leaves gone forever?

The painting disturbed her. She moved on. A girl, about twelve, painted yellow and orange sunflowers with huge bumblebees that appeared to be attacking the flowers.

Like chemo attacks cancer.

Another boy, about her brother's age, had painted a big red barn and a brown house.

"That's a really nice painting," Zoe said.

The boy looked up at her. "This is my house. I live on a farm a long, long, long way from here. I'm going to paint all our animals. We have lots and lots of animals."

Zoe looked at the big purple animal in his painting. "Oh, so you have dinosaurs on your farm?"

"No, silly. That's my dog, Shaggy."

"Oh, yeah, right. Of course."

"Do you think my dog misses me? He died and went to heaven. I miss him."

Zoe felt the air leave her lungs. "I'm sure he misses you too," she said softly, wondering where her voice had just gone. She cleared her throat. "In no time, you'll be well, and back on the farm with all your animals."

He dipped his brush in the purple paint. "But if I don't, then I'll see Shaggy again. Right?"

Zoe wanted to say something, but the words got trapped in her heart.

The room was closing in on her. She felt like she was hyperventilating. She couldn't get out of there fast enough.

"I can't do this," she said, rushing into Mr. Martinez's office.

He was holding a maple frame in one hand and a silver frame in the other, scrutinizing each before glancing at a painting of running horses on his desk.

He looked at her. "Zoe, you can do this," he said, softly.

"I thought this would be perfect for me." She paused. "I don't belong in that room."

"You do belong in that room," he said, putting down the frames.

She shook her head.

"You do," he said. "Look at me."

She looked up at him, waiting, wondering, hoping.

"You go back into that room and you do what I know you were meant to do," he said.

"But I don't know what to do."

"Then think about how you want to be," he said. "How do you want to be while you're in that room?"

And Zoe thought about it for a moment. "Well, I want to be," she said slowly, "I want to be supportive, kind, encouraging. Those kinds of things."

"Then think on those things, and in that thinking, you'll know."

Zoe sighed and stood there for a moment. A delicate space hung between them. And the silence felt comforting to her. It was as though his kind and gentle nature was wrapping around her, reassuring her.

"Thank you, Mr. Martinez," she said. "I think I'm okay now." She turned and headed for the door, but stopped. "Mr. Martinez?"

"Yes, Zoe."

"Go with the maple."

He nodded. "Good choice."

She headed back to the art therapy room, thinking on those things.

She looked around the room and noticed a dark-haired girl, about her age, painting a seascape. The sapphire sky and popcorn clouds contrasted nicely against the turquoise sea and white sailboats. The girl brushed indigo across the sky. She brushed more indigo across the turquoise sea.

No! Zoe wanted to scream. *You're ruining a beautiful piece!*

Zoe quickly approached the girl, and just as she was about to tell her that she was making it too dark, she stopped herself and thought about what Mr. Martinez had trained her to say. No criticizing. No judging. No interfering. Allow them to express as they need to express. Listen. Then listen some more.

"Is that how you feel?" Zoe asked. "That your beauty is hidden under the darkness of an illness?"

The girl stopped painting and looked up at her. "What do you mean? I'm just painting."

Zoe looked into those dark, expressive eyes. "Well, you may be painting, but what I'm seeing on the canvas may be a reflection of what's going on inside of you. Your beautiful sky and calm sea have taken on a stormy tone."

She hoped she was doing the right thing, saying the right words, and she hoped what she had just said didn't sound forced.

"I feel like that sailboat," the girl said. "A little, helpless sailboat on what was once a calm sea. I can't control the sailboat. The sea is too powerful. I'm not strong enough." She put her paintbrush down, buried her head in her hands, and sobbed.

Zoe didn't know what to do, then thought about how she had calmed Christopher whenever he cried, but then realized that putting a sock over one's hand and speaking as if she'd sucked a helium balloon was not going to work on this girl.

She took a deep breath, sat down, and then if by instinct, gently placed her hand on the girl's back. "I can't say that I know what you're going through, because I don't. I've never had a life-threatening illness, but I do know what it feels like to be scared, to feel like life is slipping out from under you, to feel sad and angry. I wish I could make things better for you, but I don't know how."

The girl wiped her tears away with the back of her hand. "My problem's not your problem. I just get angry sometimes."

"It's natural to feel that way." Zoe looked at the girl's painting. "You're good by the way."

"At what? Getting mad or painting?" the girl asked, chuckling softly. She drew a breath, a breath of strength.

"When I get out of here, I'm going to study art."

"You'd be good at that. You totally rock." Zoe stood, started to walk away, but turned back. "What's your name?"

"Hannah Perez."

"Nice to meet you, Hannah Perez."

Zoe looked into those dark, expressive eyes. Eyes full of sadness, yet hope. Eyes full of strain, yet peace. And why did she feel as though she knew Hannah from somewhere?

Chapter Fourteen

As Zoe worked with the patients-turned-artists, her confidence grew. Maybe Mr. Martinez was right. She was okay—well, better anyway. And when the patient couldn't make it to the art therapy room, she went to them. Like Nathan. He loved to paint butterflies, so every afternoon she pulled his bedside tray close to him and placed the paper, paint, and brushes on the tray, and together they created butterflies.

Zoe taped the butterfly art to the ceiling tiles directly above his bed, and slowly, the white tiles gave way to butterflies of vibrant oranges, purples, blues, and yellows. She smiled at the thought of Nathan opening his eyes every morning, looking straight up, and having something beautiful to gaze upon.

"You now have your very own ceiling of healing," she told him.

And surely, somewhere, Florence Nightingale was smiling.

Nathan wrapped his skinny arms around her, giving her

a tight squeeze, and Zoe thought he was quite strong for such a sickly child. She left Nathan to rest and to gaze upon his butterflies.

Today, she would spend time with Nina, the girl who loved painting sunflowers. In a previous session, Zoe had explained how the Fibonacci sequence comes into play with sunflowers, and how sunflowers have rows of petals in pairs of twenty-one, thirty-four, fifty-five, and eighty-nine. The seeds in its yellow head are set out in a number of spirals, usually thirty-four going one way and fifty-five going the other. "Math plus Nature equals Art," Zoe had told her, but confessed to her in the same breath how much she hated math. "Me too," Nina had said.

"Hey, Nina," Zoe said.

"Hi, Zoe."

She looked at Nina's painting. This time the flowers seemed happy to be giving to the bees what the bees needed, and the bees seemed happy to be receiving what the flowers so willingly gave. Zoe complimented her on her improvement, and Nina said, "Thanks. I'm feeling much better since I've started painting. I guess this art therapy really does work."

"No, I meant, ah, never mind," Zoe said. "I'm glad you're feeling better."

She spotted Hannah sitting a few chairs down. "Hey, Hannah, how's it going?"

Hannah didn't respond, but instead continued to stare at a blank canvas.

Zoe plopped down next to her.

"I'm trying to decide what to paint today," Hannah said, tapping her brush against the canvas with one hand while rubbing her necklace with the other. "Any ideas?"

Zoe knew that people often did touch their jewelry when anxious, apprehensive, or not feeling quite right. A twist of the ring, a twirl of the bracelet, a tug of the earring. Hannah continued to rub her necklace. Zoe thought she looked as though she was rubbing a magic lamp about to grant her a wish, and in that moment, she silently granted one for her, a wish of wellness.

Hannah dropped her hand. The necklace. A sterling silver angel with an emerald. That's it! That's where she knew Hannah. Well, not Hannah, but Hannah's mom.

Hannah's mom had come into the store. "I need a gift for my daughter," the woman had said. "She's not doing so well." Zoe remembered being impatient with the woman for taking such a long time deciding what to purchase.

She sat there for a minute, saying nothing, and now feeling terrible for not taking the time with the woman that she should have, the woman whose daughter sat next to her, the woman whose daughter was now slowly wasting away.

Then there were the other customers who were turning out to have connections to the hospital. She had suspected that Lisa Salisbury seemed familiar, and now she knew why. She had called Lisa to tell her the flowers were ready. When Lisa came to pick them up, she had told Zoe how beautiful they were, and hopefully, they would provide a ray of sunshine for a very special lady. That very special lady being Mrs. Martin! And Zoe hadn't asked, because she didn't want to know why some very special lady in her life needed a ray of sunshine. *Don't we all*, she remembered thinking.

And that picture Matt had of his girlfriend. She was the same woman who had come into the shop to buy essential oils.

Zoe suggested to Hannah that she work on her sea-scapes, then she stepped outside into the full brightness of the sun and fresh air. She took a deep cleansing breath, but the air felt stifling and her lungs so small.

How could she have been so selfish? When the customers in the shop needed her help, her empathy, she had met them with an annoyed, hurried, insensitive attitude because her thoughts weren't of helping anyone, but of Dylan. A small anthill in the crack of the sidewalk caught her attention. Even they knew how to be together, to cooperate, to help one another. She wasn't any better than an ant builder.

She stepped back into the hospital, and as much as she wanted to check on Hannah, she decided who she really needed to see was Maggie.

Maggie's office door was slightly open. Zoe peered in. Her aunt was sitting on the edge of her desk, and a man stood in front of her, close. Zoe recognized him as the man who had bumped into her on her first day of community service here. She decided now was not a good time, but as she was about to leave, the man looked up at her.

"You have a visitor," he said.

"I can come back," Zoe said, glancing from the man to Maggie.

Maggie met her glance with a deer-in-the-headlights look.

"I was just leaving," the man said, stepping away from Maggie.

Maggie jumped off her desk and straightened her skirt. "Zoe, this is Dr. Scott Swanson. Scott, this is my niece, Zoe."

He smiled. "I believe we've met."

Zoe nodded.

"You're doing much better since last I saw you," he said.

"I am. Thanks."

He turned to Maggie. "I need to be going. I have patients waiting, but be sure to keep me posted."

"I will."

"Nice to see you again, Zoe," he said, before heading out the door.

Zoe wasn't so sure she shouldn't leave too. The air in the room seemed heavy and stifled, as though a storm had just passed and now all that remained was a small electrical charge.

"I'm sorry I interrupted your meeting," Zoe said.

A meeting of the hearts.

Her aunt straightened some manila file folders on her desk, folders that didn't need straightening. "No need to apologize."

But when she spoke, it sounded more like, *What do you think you're doing interrupting me like that?*

Zoe needed Maggie's support now more than ever and hoped her aunt would understand. She desperately needed for someone to, but perhaps she should leave and go back to the art room and forget asking her the question that had been haunting her for weeks.

Maggie tossed the file folders into her desk drawer. "Is everything okay with the patients in the art room?"

Artists.

"It's all good."

"I knew you'd be a good fit for that program." Maggie motioned for Zoe to have a seat. "Now, what's on your mind?" she said, relaxing into her desk chair.

"Aunt Maggie, do you believe a person can die and then come back?"

Zoe thought Maggie was contemplating this question for far too long, and Zoe was about to say never mind and leave. But Maggie finally spoke.

"Yes, I do," she said, softly. "It's about the only thing that keeps me sane in an insane world. If I didn't believe in reincarnation, the law of karma, the evolution of the soul as it makes its many journeys, well, I think this thing we call life would be almost too unbearable at times."

Reincarnation? Who said anything about reincarnation?

Zoe shook her head, rubbed her eyes, and looked up at Maggie. "No, I wasn't talking about that. I meant when a person dies and that same person comes back, back into their own body in this life."

She desperately hoped Maggie understood this time.

Maggie leaned forward, resting her forearms on her desk. "You mean a near-death experience?"

Zoe nodded.

"I've talked with patients who've had them," Maggie said.

"You have?"

Maggie nodded.

"I think you're about to talk with someone else who's had one." She paused. "Me."

She searched Maggie's eyes for an indication of not being crazy. She thought she caught a glimmer of knowing in her aunt's eyes, and that was all the assurance she needed. "Well, I don't think I had one," she said. "I know I had one."

Maggie eyes diverted away from her to a pen on her desk, and as she stared at the pen, a look of guilt seemed to sweep across her face.

It's a stupid pen, Maggie. It's not going to write the response for you.

Maggie finally looked up. "Zoe, I read your medical chart from your car accident."

"What?"

"I'll admit it wasn't ethical," she said, raising her hand as if taking a solemn vow that she'd never do it again, "but I felt I had to." She paused. "You flatlined."

"I did what?"

"You died, Zoe."

The words slowly rolled around in Zoe's head, and her brain cells did a *snap, crackle, pop* as she processed what Maggie had just said. So it hadn't been a dream. It hadn't been the drugs. It hadn't been her imagination. Her experience had been real, a truth she had felt all along, but grew tired of battling everyone about, so she had dismissed it as an untruth. It was real. It was something real.

"Why didn't anyone tell me? Am I brain damaged or something and don't even know it?"

Maggie chuckled. "No, you're not brain damaged. You're

fine. Well, we think you are, anyway," she said, grinning. "And as for your mom and Charles not telling you, well, I shouldn't speak for them, but perhaps they felt that you needed time to recover."

Zoe sat there, feeling dumbfounded.

"What is it?" Maggie asked.

"How could they know that I flatlined, but yet not believe me when I told them that I had some weird, yet totally awesome, experience with Grandma? Isn't that what people do when they flatline? Have a near-death experience?"

"Not all do, Zoe, and not all believe." Maggie reached into her desk drawer, pulled out a business card, and handed it to her.

Zoe looked at the card: Dr. Joanna Carmichael, Near-Death Experience Support Group. "What's this?"

"A group of kids," Maggie said, "about your age. Some older. Some younger. They meet every Wednesday evening. They'll help you understand your near-death experience and what you've been through, what you'll continue to go through."

"What I'll continue to go through?" Zoe asked.

"That's why the support group," Maggie said. "It'll help you adjust to this new way of being."

As Zoe left Maggie's office, confusion swept over her. A new way of being? Great. Like life couldn't be any more difficult to figure out than it already was. And yet, she felt lighter, exuberant, and the more she thought about it, the more she looked forward to that first meeting. She wasn't the only one. She wasn't the only one!

But as she made her way to her car, she wondered what she would tell her mom and Charles. That she was going to counseling for kids who've had a near-death experience? They didn't believe she had even had one. Nobody did. Except Maggie.

As she drove home, she decided that she would tell them that she had decided to attend drug and alcohol counseling, and as soon as she got home, she told them just that, and they were pleased.

Zoe wondered how lying could be so easy, too easy. The ease of the lie bothered her. The lie itself bothered her.

And she also wondered why it was so hard for them to believe the truth, and yet so easy for them to believe a lie?

Chapter Fifteen

Zoe turned off the ignition and popped a peppermint, not only to freshen up her breath, but also to calm her stomach. She tapped her fingers on the steering wheel and debated whether or not she should forget about this and leave.

Maggie had told her to look for the wall of Leyland cypress a few yards back from the street. The entrance is narrow, so narrow that it's easy to miss. Had it not been for the cypress, Zoe figured she would have been driving up and down the street all night, a street she had traveled many times going to and from the hospital.

She looked up at the salmon-colored stucco building with its massive front windows and arched front door, and she thought it looked more like a house than an office, and she also thought the parking lot rather accommodating for so few cars. She began to wonder if perhaps Aunt Maggie hadn't told her the truth. Maybe it would be just her and the doctor.

Maybe I really am crazy, and Aunt Maggie thinks so too!

She took a deep breath and grabbed her tote.

Rows of English lavender bushes adorned the long cobbled walkway leading up to the front door, and the lavender swayed in the warm summer breeze, filling the air with an intoxicating, sweet smell. Zoe immediately felt relaxed as she opened the door and stepped inside.

She followed the sound of voices and laughter down a hallway and around a corner. She stopped at the doorway and peered in at a group of kids, actually relieved now knowing that it wouldn't be just her and the doctor. She observed the kids for a moment talking, laughing, a toss of the hair, a pat on the back, sipping drinks, munching on cookies, a smile, a hug, another warm embrace. They all seemed so comfortable with one another and she felt a little uncomfortable at how comfortable they did seem, as though they had all been friends forever and here she was, the odd kid, and why did she suddenly feel like an intruder.

She decided this was stupid. She didn't belong here. She would get in her car and go somewhere, anywhere to kill time, and then go home and tell her parents how her first counseling session went. She turned and walked back down the hallway, and just as she was about to round the corner, she heard a soft, warm voice.

"Hi. You must be Zoe."

A high alert sounded in Zoe's brain. Should she pretend not to have heard her and keep walking? Or lie and tell her she's mistaken. She's not Zoe. And leave. Just leave. But the voice was so soft. So warm. So kind and gentle that Zoe couldn't help but to turn around.

A willowy woman, wearing an ankle-length denim skirt, white bohemian blouse, and turquoise necklace, extended her hand to her. A silver strand of hair had come loose from her bun and was now brushing across her shoulder.

"I'm Joanna," she said, her blue-gray eyes sparkling. "Maggie's told me about you."

Zoe wondered what exactly Maggie had told her. That she was a nutcase in desperate need of some serious therapy?

"Go on in and make yourself at home, and be sure to help yourself to the refreshments. We'll be starting shortly." And with that, Joanna slipped back into her office.

Feeling defeated, Zoe headed back to the room. She stood at the entrance for a moment, afraid to take that first step.

I don't have to come back. I'll just stay for this one meeting and that's it. I think I can make it through one. If not, then I'll leave during the break and never see any of these people again.

Then she wondered if they even took a break.

She entered the room and beelined to the refreshment table—no hellos to anyone, no eye contact, just get to the refreshment table. She grabbed a plate and a napkin and looked over the assortment of chips, cheeses, crackers, and cookies.

"My mom made the oatmeal raisin cookies. They're really good."

Zoe looked over her shoulder. A boy, about ten years old, munched on an oatmeal raisin cookie. She suspected that this boy probably ate many cookies. His chubby, rosy cheeks lit upon an angelic face, and his striped T-shirt fit snugly over his tummy.

"Well, I don't particularly care for oatmeal raisin," Zoe said, trying to sound pleasant, knowing that offending his mom's baking might forfeit a good first impression.

"Oh, then try the chocolate chip. They're delicious," he said, taking another bite of his cookie.

She reached for a chocolate chip cookie, then poured herself a glass of juice.

The boy munched away on his cookie.

"You're new, huh?" he said.

Zoe nodded.

"Hey, don't be scared."

And how did he know she was? Was it because her hand shook when she had poured herself the glass of juice, or because she had dropped her napkin and then spilled some juice when she went to pick it up?

"Joanna's really nice," he said. "The whole group's nice."

Zoe bent down to wipe up the spill.

"Hey, Squirt."

Zoe glanced up at the person who had called the boy Squirt and who was now tousling his hair. He wore a letter jacket, and Zoe recognized the high school as Rock Ridge's rival from across town. His football jersey fit snug, as did his jeans. His short, spiked blond hair emphasized his cool blue eyes, which sparkled with good humor. He flashed a wide, white smile and his cheeks dimpled.

The boy turned around and dryly said, "Gabriel, you know I hate it when you do that."

"Ah, come on, Michael. You know I'm just playing around."

Zoe tossed the napkin into the trash. When she looked back up, she caught Gabriel's eye and she felt a breath catch in her throat. She felt as though he wasn't looking at her, but through her.

"Hey, who's your new friend?" he asked, turning his gaze back to Michael.

"What's your name?" Michael asked.

"Zoe."

Gabriel stepped past Michael and extended his hand to Zoe. "Nice to meet you, Zoe, and welcome. So, NDEer?"

"Huh?"

"Short for near-death experience," Michael explained.

"Ah, yeah, I'm an NDEer," said Zoe. "When you say it like that, it almost sounds like a disease." She laughed nervously.

Gabriel and Michael both stared at her.

Okay, awkward. Not making progress so much.

"So, Zoe," Gabriel said, "what gift did you get?"

"Excuse me?" Zoe asked, glancing from Gabriel to Michael.

"Gabriel," said Michael, "you know it's against the rules to ask."

"Mine's time travel," Gabriel said.

"Time travel?" Zoe asked.

Gabriel laughed. "Nah, just messing with you. Nobody can do that. Well, at least we don't think so."

Michael rolled his eyes. "Zoe, don't pay any attention to him. Come on, they're about to start. You can sit next to me."

As they walked toward the sofa, Zoe whispered to Michael, "What did he mean by what gift did you get?"

"You'll see," Michael said.

Zoe wasn't so certain she wanted to see. Maybe now was a good time to leave, but Michael looked up at her and smiled such a wonderful, innocent smile that taking a seat next to him on the sofa seemed like the most natural thing to do.

All of the kids took a seat and introduced themselves. Zoe figured it was standard procedure because she was certain all these kids knew each other already. A girl, about seven, introduced herself as Emily, then she introduced her look-a-like doll, Faith.

Two more girls, a year or two younger than Zoe, introduced themselves as Jamie and Melissa. Jamie told how she'd been coming to the meetings for about three years and went on to say how she couldn't imagine not having this support group. Melissa stated how she'd been coming for about one year, and she, too, mentioned how invaluable the group had been in helping her deal with her near-death experience. Zoe wondered what exactly she was dealing with.

Most of them had been coming for less than three years, and Zoe wondered if perhaps that was the cutoff point. If a person didn't get it together after three years of having had a totally weird experience, then they'd never get it together, and then why bother continuing, and she wondered how long before she'd no longer come. Probably after tonight.

Then it was her turn, and why did she feel awkward when all eyes suddenly looked at her? She glanced at Joanna as though getting her permission before speaking. Joanna smiled. Zoe smiled a faint smile back.

"Hi everyone. I'm Zoe, and I had what I think was, no, it was a near-death experience, and yeah, I guess that's why I'm here." She paused, not sure how to continue. She looked at the eyes looking at her. They were kind eyes, supportive eyes. "My aunt thought it would be a good idea."

Oh, god, how lame was that?

She looked at Joanna with a look that asked, *Do you need for me to say anything else, or was that good enough?*

Joanna smiled. "Welcome, Zoe."

And the group said, "Welcome, Zoe."

Zoe smiled a hesitant smile. Joanna asked if anyone had any questions for Zoe. One girl asked her what high school she went to, another girl asked her what she likes to do for fun, and Michael asked her what her favorite food was. Zoe answered all their questions with Rock Ridge High, shopping (she didn't dare say partying), and lasagna (her mom's).

Zoe felt exhausted, and when Joanna said, "Enough questions, let's move on," Zoe was relieved. She exhaled.

Joanna began by talking about divine energy, and while it may not always seem like it, the Universe is on our side, always there rooting for us in its infinite patience and wisdom and love.

Zoe didn't feel so sure about that universe thing. It never felt that way to her, especially when she was a child, and her mom and her biological father fought while she lay in bed, palms cupped over ears, humming to drain it all out. She had imagined angels in her room comforting her, taking the pain from her, and flying away with it. The universe was on our side. Did these kids really believe that?

She listened as they talked about their lives following their near-death experience, the gifts they had received, the gifts that Michael had apparently meant when he said, "You'll see."

Melissa revealed how her hearing was especially acute now, almost to the point of being irritating.

That's a gift that could actually come in handy.

A young boy, who had introduced himself as Stephen, could now see music as color.

"It's way cool when I play my violin to see all those beautiful colors swirling all around," he said. "Although, sometimes it can be distracting."

Hallucinations, anyone?

One could communicate telepathically, some were now psychic, some had the ability to perform hands-on healings. But not one mentioned time travel.

She wondered if now might be a good time to sneak out, but she happened to glance over at Gabriel, who had the sweetest countenance about him. He gave her a quick nod and smile, so beautiful, so encouraging, so warm that she couldn't bring herself to leave. She decided she liked him even if he was a jock. She didn't know why, other than they shared a common bond of having had a near-death experience. She wondered why he hadn't mentioned his gift, but then figured he probably had in previous sessions.

She continued to listen as some of the older kids talked about struggling with their gifts and their new sense of self, but the younger ones seemed more okay with their gifts. What most weren't okay with was the lack of understanding or not being believed. Strained family relationships were common. Friendships ended, but they reassured one another that they now had new friends who did understand them and who did believe them. To be understood and to be believed. What more could a kid ask for?

Joanna wrapped up the meeting by saying, "Stay safe and have a good week."

Zoe thanked her for the meeting.

Joanna said, "I'll see you next week."

Zoe nodded and slipped out without saying good-bye to anyone. She thought she heard Michael call her name.

Those kids are nothing like me. They're crazy. What was Maggie thinking sending me to a support group like that?

While driving home, she thought about those words Maggie had uttered: "A situation in the oncology department." The situation must have something to do with her, or Maggie wouldn't have bothered moving her to the art program. And what were those two men doing lurking around the hospital?

She would have to ask Maggie about that situation next time she saw her, but first she had a little situation of her own to figure out. And she would. Tomorrow.

Chapter Sixteen

Zoe held the barcode scanner and scanned the angels. She scanned the jewelry, herbs, pots, and water features. She scanned the cards and stationery, and all the while thought of Dylan. Was he seeing someone else?

A few days ago, she saw two teenage girls enter the bookstore. They walked arm in arm, laughing and giggling. How they could be so happy about going into a bookstore? Were they in there flirting with him? Did he read poetry to them like he had read it to her? Was that his deal? Read them poetry?

Why hadn't he called or texted? Said something. Anything. Maybe he thought she didn't want to see him. She needed him to know that wasn't the case. Did he want to see her? If he didn't want to see her anymore, she could handle that, couldn't she?

"How are you coming on inventory?" her mom asked, herb snips in hand.

Zoe dropped the barcode scanner. "I have two more shelves to do," she said. "Then I'm done."

"With inventory," Mom said. "Then I'd like you to redo that front window. For god's sake, Zoe, this isn't a funeral parlor."

"It's dramatic," Zoe said.

"It's depressing," Mom said. "Redo it." She grabbed an herb plant and retreated to the back room.

Zoe yanked the indigo gossamer down and wondered if she and her mom would ever see eye to eye on anything. She draped a light blue fabric across the top of the window, allowing it to fall freely down the frame. She tied yellow ribbons at the top corners. She replaced the bouquet of deep purple and velvety maroon tulips with pink calla lilies and positioned the bouquet in the center of the window. She stepped back and looked at the display. Baby shower, anyone?

She glanced across the street at the Abyss Bookstore. The red OPEN sign blinked on and off. Was Dylan even working today? She needed to find out.

She told her mom she was taking a quick break, then headed across the street to the bookstore. The smell of dusty paperbacks filled the air, and the floorboards creaked under her. A gray-haired man behind the counter peered over the paperback he was reading. "Good afternoon, miss. Looking for anything special?"

"Just looking."

She moved down an aisle, then another, and another.

"Um, sir, excuse me," she said, popping her head up over a bookshelf.

"Yes?" the man said, licking his finger before flipping to the next page.

"Do you have any books on near-death experiences?"

"Last bookshelf at the end," he replied, not taking his eyes off the paperback, but simply pointing to a far corner.

She scanned the books on that corner shelf, running her fingers along the spines. She pulled out a book by Dr. P. M. H. Atwater on near-death experiences and the aftereffects and thumbed through it. It looked promising. Another book by Edgar Cayce on reincarnation caught her eye. She knew she didn't have enough money for both, so which one? She plopped down on the floor and read the chapter headings from each book.

"Can I help you find something?"

A familiar voice. The black boots he wore were so close she could reach out and touch them.

She looked up. "Dylan?"

"Zoe? Wow, what a surprise."

"Yeah," she said, standing. "What a surprise."

She tried to sound thrilled, but instead surprised herself with how she actually did sound. Scared. Nervous. And how she felt. Awkward. Timid. And she wondered where she had gone just now.

"I almost didn't recognize you," he said, pointing to her hair.

"Different, huh?"

"I like it." He took a step back. "And you've lost a lot of weight. Not that you needed to," he quickly added.

Zoe grinned.

A delicate silence hung in the air.

"I did call you," Dylan said. "Once, but your mom answered, so I hung up. I didn't try again."

"It's okay," Zoe said.

A lie.

He brushed his finger against her arm. "I did come to the hospital to see you."

"You did?"

"When I asked the gal at the front desk where your room was, she asked me if I was family, and I said yes. I guess I must have hesitated too long. She wouldn't let me pass. I didn't dare go to your house or walk over to the shop."

"You came to the hospital?"

He nodded. "I know you got messed up pretty bad because my mom called your mom to see how you were. My mom told me that your mom said that she didn't want me around you anymore." He shrugged. "So I stayed away, but I want you to know I didn't want to."

She suddenly felt at a loss for words. She remembered how she had cursed him a thousand times for not calling, not stopping by, not seeing how she was when all this time he had. She felt sad, but at the same time angry—angry at her mom and Charles for not telling her that Dylan's mom had called and for not allowing him to see her in the hospital.

"I probably wouldn't have remembered you being there, anyway," Zoe said.

She looked at her books and felt that perhaps now would be a good time to leave. She didn't think she would feel so sad seeing Dylan again. She wished time travel really did exist, but not physical time travel. Emotional time travel. She had desperately wanted to see him, and now as she stood in front of him, she felt as though she no longer cared. Well, she did, but not as much as she thought she would have.

"What have you got there?" Dylan asked, breaking the awkward silence. He reached out, and she handed him the books. He stared at the covers, thumbed through the pages, then flipped the books over and glanced at the back cover. "You don't really believe in this stuff, do you?"

"I'm not sure what I believe, but I thought these books might help."

"Help with what?"

She shrugged. "Just stuff."

Why suddenly did she feel like Hester Prynne standing on the scaffold, Hester who probably wanted to scream at the Puritans for judging and ostracizing her, to scream so loudly that the sound she made carried through the village, through the forest, and into the heavens. Zoe wanted to scream, too, and scream so loud that her sound traveled all the way to the heavens. All the way to Grandma.

He held up the book on reincarnation. "So, we come back as animals or something?"

Before she could tell him how stupid that sounded, he continued, "Because if I came back as an animal, I think I'd want to be a gazelle for speed. Or maybe a dolphin. They always seem to be having so much fun. But not a dolphin at those water parks. A dolphin free in the ocean. Or maybe a pig for intelligence. Wait, maybe not. I'd be sacrificed for food or for human parts. You know the DNA of a pig closely matches the DNA of a human. Too close if you ask me. Too close to be eating."

"We don't come back as animals," she said. "We come back as another person, and hopefully, better than the one before."

"So you do believe in this crap," he said.

"I don't know what I believe right now," she said, the heat rising in her face, "but at least I'm being open-minded."

Dylan rolled his eyes and handed the books back to her. She took the books into her trembling hands. Why did she suddenly feel as though the bookshelves were closing in and that it wouldn't be long before the shelves toppled and the books tumbled right down on her?

She held up the book by Dr. P. M. H. Atwater. "I think I had one of these."

"A what?"

"A near-death experience."

He looked at her, a sideways look. "How hard did the doctors say you hit your head?"

She clutched the books to her chest and leaned into him. "Well, if we did come back as an animal, you'd come back as a jackass. Oh, wait, you already are!"

She threw the books down and ran out. She wanted to slam the door, but decided she was better than that. And she also decided that for a poetry-reading guy, he sure was a jerk.

She hurried back to the flower shop and wiped away her tears. She couldn't cry. Not now. Not in front of her mom or the customers. She busied her mind by straightening the shelves, wondering why customers couldn't put things back the way they'd found them.

And while straightening the shelves, she thought about the meeting the night before. She felt confused and didn't know whether or not to go back. She should at least have bought one of those books. But meeting or no meeting, book or no book, how was she going to make it through another week without feeling as though everything she thought she knew was about to come crashing down?

Chapter Seventeen

Zoe sat on her bed shading in the long, dark tresses of her princess warrior. Her princess stood proudly on a ridge overlooking a city in the distance, a city she would soon conquer. Zoe held up her drawing and decided she liked her princess with her form-fitting leather dress. She smiled at her ability to capture such intensity in her dark eyes, an intensity that spoke of cataclysmic disaster for the enemy, but with those eyes and her tresses, her princess could easily go from day warrior to night seductress. A different kind of conquering.

She placed her drawing on her easel, a sweet-sixteen birthday present from Nicole, then ran downstairs and into the kitchen. She poured herself a glass of juice, and just as she was about to take a drink, the phone rang. She answered it.

"Hello," she said.

"You left without saying good-bye."

"Of course I left without saying good-bye. You were an ass. A total ass."

Silence.

"Dylan?"

"Ah, no."

Zoe's eyes grew wide. Her heart skipped a beat. She felt her face flush. She wanted to hang up. She didn't care who it was.

"It's Gabriel," he said, softly. "From the meeting."

"Oh, my god, I am so sorry. I thought—"

"Hey, nothing to be sorry about. I should have told you who was calling. I got your number from Joanna. I hope you don't mind."

"No, not at all."

"I was wondering if you had any questions or concerns about your first meeting."

Her head was spinning. Questions? Yeah, she had a lot of them. She poked her head around the corner. Mom and Charles were watching *Antiques Roadshow*. One of the Keno brothers was appraising a table. Her mom's favorite. Keno brother, that is. Zoe could ask plenty of questions now. She wouldn't be interrupted anytime soon. But she didn't know what to ask.

"Um, no," she finally said. "I don't have any questions."

A gap hung on the other end. Zoe wondered if he had heard her, if she should say something, but she wasn't sure what to say. She decided a "thanks" would be appropriate, which she was about to say and then hang up, but he continued, "I also called because I want you to know that if you don't want to come back next Wednesday, that's okay, but I hope your aunt told you about the agreement."

"Agreement?" she asked with a nervous chuckle, anticipating a punch line.

"Whether you come back or not, you aren't to tell anyone about the meetings." He paused. "Ever."

Gulp.

Why hadn't her aunt told her that before she agreed to go to one? She probably never would have gone in the first place. But then, no one believed that she'd had a near-death experience anyway, so what would it matter if she inadvertently blurted out that she attended meetings for kids who died and came back and now had all kinds of weird gifts.

All she could squeak out was, "Okay."

She hung up the phone, and when her mom, eyes glued to her show, asked who had called, Zoe told her it was Hailey wanting to know when they could go shopping for school clothes.

Her mom turned around and looked at her. "Hailey's back from Texas already?"

"Ah, yeah, I guess her grandma got kind of sick so she came home early."

"I hope her grandmother is okay," Mom said, turning back to her show. She turned around again and looked at Zoe. "Maybe we could send Hailey a card?"

"That would be nice," Charles said.

"Ah, no," Zoe said. "I mean, yes. I'll take care of it."

She didn't like lying to her mom and Charles about that phone call or about Hailey's grandmother, but what else could she do?

***

Wednesday night had rolled around, and Zoe contemplated whether or not she wanted to attend another NDE meeting. Either way, though, she had to leave the house. She had a ruse to keep up. She'd go to Isabelle's band concert. That would be a nice way to spend the evening. She called her house.

"She's at summer band camp, dear," Isabelle's mom said.

"Oh, yeah, I forgot about that."

"You can write to her. I'm sure she'd like hearing from you."

"I'll do that. Thanks."

Zoe grabbed her car keys and headed out the door. She had to go somewhere, and she wondered why she felt so conflicted about going to another meeting. Was it because the seemingly normal kids weren't so normal after all? That she had nothing in common with them? That she felt like an intruder?

She knew she should at least apologize to Gabriel for calling him an ass, although it really wasn't Gabriel she had meant to call an ass. Then she wondered about Dylan and what he was doing, and then she wondered why she even cared, and why did she feel like her head was about to explode?

She drove past the Abyss Bookstore. She didn't know why she did, because she knew it was closed. She wondered for a split second where Dylan lived. She didn't even know where he lived. Maybe that was a good thing. With her luck, he'd be out front. He'd see her and she'd feel like an idiot. Then she realized how pathetic that all was. And she decided right then that she was not going to be pathetic. Not with Dylan and not with Gabriel. And, not with herself. With that thought, she drove to the center. She would apologize to Gabriel and then tell him and Joanna that she wouldn't be returning and that she understood she was not to tell anyone about the meetings.

Once inside, she spotted Gabriel standing by the refreshment table, water bottle in hand. She was about to approach him, but the way he interacted with the kids gave her pause. He seemed so at ease with them. They all seemed to hang on his every word, especially Michael, even if Gabriel did call him Squirt and tousle his hair.

Who was he really? She knew she'd never find out, because in a few short minutes, she'd be in her car driving aimlessly around again. She walked toward him, but Emily bounded toward her and wrapped her arms around her.

"You came back," she said.

Jamie and Melissa ran up and gave her a warm hug. One by one, all of the kids welcomed her back, and between hugs she wondered how she was going to explain to them that she wasn't there to stay.

Stephen welcomed her with a high five, and she high-fived him back, feeling slightly awkward at his enthusiastic friendliness.

Michael approached her with a plate of chocolate chip cookies, and when she took one, she noticed how her hand didn't shake, and in that moment, she wondered if perhaps she did belong here with these kids.

Melissa said, "Welcome back. It's good to see you again. I

hope we didn't freak you out about our gifts, though."

Zoe smiled a weak smile and said, "Ah, no, it's all good. No worries." But at the same time, doubt crept in. Did she belong here with them? After all, she didn't have a gift. Only the near-death experience to connect her with these kids. Why was she beginning to feel like that intruder all over again?

"Sit by me and Melissa tonight," Jamie said.

And just like that, the intruder tiptoed away.

Gabriel approached Zoe. "I need to apologize," he said, "I shouldn't have—"

"You don't need to apologize," Zoe said. "I'm the one who should apologize for the other night."

He flashed a warm smile. "Remind me to never get on your bad side."

Jamie and Melissa looked at one another, then at Zoe as if wanting her to offer up the details of the other night.

"Something we should know about?" Melissa asked.

"No!" they both said, lightheartedly.

"Come on," Jamie said. "I think the meeting is about to start."

Zoe grabbed herself a glass of lemonade before settling in on the sofa between Melissa and Jamie. A few kids sat on large meditation pillows and some in beanbag chairs. The sound of water gently cascading down rocks and the soft lighting of the crystal salt lamps relaxed Zoe even more. Funny, she hadn't noticed the water feature or the lamps in the last meeting. She suddenly felt very peaceful, like space and time had never separated her from these kids.

Joanna asked who would like to begin. Emily raised her hand. Joanna nodded in encouragement.

"Faith had a near-death experience," Emily said, holding up her doll.

No one laughed. They all looked at her in support. They knew that sometimes Emily had to speak to them about her own experience through her doll. Emily told them about how she and Faith met Saint Germain and how nice he was and how he took her hand and Faith's hand and gave them each a purple iris, telling them that they now had their very own link between heaven and earth.

Zoe thought Emily's experience was incredibly intriguing, awe inspiring. But seriously? She had spoken to Saint Germain? For such a young girl, she was so articulate. Zoe now felt like she had sounded like a babbling idiot. No wonder no one in her family believed her.

One girl told how her near-death experience felt scary, like being swallowed up into a cold, dark hole. Zoe felt surprise and confusion. She had assumed that all near-death experiences were good and beautiful.

A few expressed how they still weren't comfortable talking about the details of their experience or of their gift. Joanna replied with, "It's not about something happening *to* you. It's about something happening *for* you. We're not here to get what we want necessarily, but what we need."

Joanna proceeded to talk more about the benevolent universe supporting us and guiding us on our path, gently calling us to expand in our awareness of truth and love. Not much of this made any sense to Zoe, but at least this meeting didn't have too many new and weird surprises. That was the last thing she needed.

Joanna closed the meeting with, "Namaste."

"Namaste," they all said.

Namaste?

"Hey, Zoe," Gabriel said, approaching her. "I just wanted to tell you that I'm glad you decided to come back. Everyone is."

"Me too," she said. "Really glad."

She wondered how she could have underestimated these kids and their ability to make her feel at home, a feeling she hadn't felt since the accident. Incident. Whatever. She was wrong once again. She did need this group.

"I have a surprise," Gabriel said, reaching into a cooler of icy slush and grabbing another water. He wiped his wet hand off on his jeans. "Well, I don't know if it's a surprise or not, but I put in for a school transfer and it went through. I'll be attending my senior year at Rock Ridge High."

"What?" she said, choking down her lemonade. She coughed and patted her chest. "You're kidding, right?" She coughed some more.

"You okay?"

She nodded.

"I guess I did surprise you, huh?"

"Yeah," she said, her voice a few octaves higher. She cleared her throat. "The lemonade is especially tart."

Gabriel laughed and held up his water to her glass.

"That's great, Gabriel," she said, tapping her glass to his bottled water.

He took a swig. "I needed a change, a fresh start. I think it'll be a good move for me. My parents think so too."

Zoe wasn't too certain she wanted to know why he needed a change. She wanted to ask, but he continued, "If anything happens, I got your back."

What was he talking about? Did she even want to know? She could take care of herself, couldn't she?

"Thanks," she said, hoping that he didn't detect the confusion in her voice.

Not only did she now feel better about starting her junior year, but she also felt better about the support group. But even so, why did she feel like something was off, amiss, and that when she figured out what that something was, it would be too late. She brushed off the thought.

Before leaving this time, she said good-bye to everyone, to all of her new friends.

Life was good.

Confusing, but good.

Chapter Eighteen

Zoe sat on the front porch swing reading a poem in *Teen Ink* magazine, which expressed the angst of friendships changing over time, a common topic in her Wednesday night support group, but as much as she tried, thoughts of Hailey fogged her ability to concentrate. She was excited about seeing her today, yet nervous. So much had happened over the summer. How would she even begin to tell her everything?

Of course, she couldn't tell her everything. Not about the Wednesday night meetings, which she had been attending faithfully now for about a month. She was sworn to secrecy, so she shouldn't feel too bad about not saying anything to Hailey.

Mom and Charles had told her how pleased they were at how committed she was to her alcohol and drug counseling, and she told them she was glad too. She told them very little about the other kids in the group, about their own personal struggles, and definitely not one word about their gifts.

She had become better acquainted with the kids. Emily, with her look-alike doll that she carried everywhere along with a security blanket; Stephen, who dreamed of being a classical violinist someday; and Jamie; and Melissa; and Michael; and Gabriel; and all the others. Zoe had decided that those kids weren't so crazy after all. Because if they were, then what was she?

The music of Taylor Swift blaring on the radio and a *beep-beep-beep* of a horn brought her out of her reverie. She looked up.

"Hailey!"

She tossed her magazine onto the swing and ran down the front porch steps.

"Zoe!" Hailey said, getting out of her dad's rusted-out Ford truck.

They embraced in a warm hug.

Hailey took a step back to look at her friend. "Your hair!" she said, taking a lock of Zoe's hair and running it through her fingers. "It looks great. You look great, and you've lost so much weight."

Friends are so good for the ego.

"Thanks, Hailey. You look pretty awesome yourself. I guess Texas was good to you."

"Texas was hot and humid, but so good for the hair and skin, so unlike Colorado," she said as they climbed into the truck, "which I much prefer, actually. Texas sucks. Except for the grandparents, of course."

Hailey continued to talk about Dallas and her grandparents and their horse ranch as she drove out of the neighborhood and onto a main street, which would take them to the historic district.

"Have you heard from Isabelle much this summer?" Hailey asked.

"She doesn't get back from band camp until tomorrow," Zoe said.

"Okay, then tomorrow night we par-taaay!" She slurped her soda and sped through a yellow-turned-red light.

Someone honked.

"Learn how to drive yourself!" Hailey yelled out the window.

But the thought of partying didn't thrill Zoe, nor the drinking or the drugging. In fact, she hadn't had a drink or any weed since the accident. She hadn't really thought about it. She wasn't so sure she liked this person she was becoming. It scared her. But why?

Hailey sucked the last of her soda through the straw with a long gurgling sound. "So, how was your summer?"

"Life's been good," Zoe said. "Doing the community service thing at the hospital and working at the shop. It's all good."

Hailey turned onto Mountain View Avenue. "Why do I feel like you're not telling me something?"

"Dylan and I broke up."

"Damn, Zoe. Okay, all the more reason to party when Isabelle gets back."

They passed the German bakery, the theater, and the candle shop, and as they passed the Abyss Bookstore, Zoe looked over her shoulder and stared and stared and stared.

Hailey glanced over her shoulder. "Since when are you into books?" she asked, but before Zoe could answer, Hailey said, "Hey, we could stop in your mom's shop and say hi."

Zoe turned back around. "Are you kidding me? My mom gave me the day off so we could go shopping. She'd probably change her mind with those sales she's having today and put me to work. You too."

"Way bad idea, then."

Hailey pulled into the parking lot of the vintage clothing store. Once inside, Zoe searched through racks and racks of tops, then rummaged through the tables, tossing aside tops that carried the potential for being labeled dorky. She tossed a few more tops, then tossed some more.

"Hey," Hailey said, gently touching Zoe's arm, "if we don't find something here, we can always go to the mall."

Zoe let out a heavy sigh. "Do you think my scar and limp are all that noticeable?"

"Zoe, I don't think you have to worry about the kids at school teasing you. Besides, it couldn't be much worse than last year, could it?"

Zoe leaned against the table. "You're probably right. I mean, what could be worse than hearing the lovely humming of the *Addams Family* theme song by Vanessa Wellington and the Gospel Girl Gang as yours truly walks down the school hall, hearing the perfect rhythmic snapping of their fingers—except for Meagan, who can't snap her fingers to save her life, so she had to resort to softly tapping on the locker instead."

"At least she did tap softly," Hailey said, grinning. "Sorry, but it was kind of funny." She held up a short denim skirt with a huge rhinestone peace symbol covering the front.

"Who would wear this?"

She laughed and laughed and tossed it back on the table, and Zoe thought the laugh sounded like residue laughter, the kind of laughter someone does when what they really want to do is laugh at what they know isn't funny to their friend, so in order to spare their feelings they don't laugh, but they can't help themselves, so they invent a situation so they can laugh. Like holding up a denim skirt emblazoned with rhinestones.

They moved away from the tables and over to a rack of tops.

"Hopefully," Hailey said, "they've run out of ideas."

"Hopefully," Zoe said, "they've grown up."

"Besides," Hailey said, "you don't even look like Wednesday Addams anymore."

Zoe leaned her hand against the rack. "I wouldn't have looked like Wednesday Addams if you hadn't left the hair dye on so long."

"I wouldn't have left the dye on so long if we hadn't been stoned, which, by the way, was your idea."

Hailey was right. It was Zoe's idea. She wasn't too sure if maybe weed wasn't overrated after all. She pushed tops to the side to get a better look at a pink T-shirt. She held it up and read the psychedelic wording, *Foxy Lady*.

Hailey glanced over. "That's lame, Zoe."

She hung it back up.

"How about this one?" Hailey asked, holding up a black tank top with the word *Paris* scripted across a red windmill.

Zoe lightly touched Hailey's arm. "Promise me," she

said. "Promise me we'll stick together no matter what."

"Zoe, we always have. Why would this year be any different?" Hailey searched through the rack. "Here you go. Extra small for you, medium for me." She handed her the tank top. "At least no one will be calling you Doughy Zoe anymore."

Zoe held up the top. "You sure this is going to fit me?"

"Hell, yeah, you skinny, totally hot, sexy bitch, you."

Zoe smiled. "I knew there was a reason you were my best friend."

"Best friends forever!" Hailey said.

They purchased their matching tops, and rhinestone bracelets and barrettes, and on the way back home, they listened to Taylor Swift's "Fifteen." Zoe only half-listened to the song and to Hailey's endless chatter about *thank god we're no longer fifteen, didn't being fifteen suck, guys are so lame at that age*, and on and on and on.

Zoe's thoughts were elsewhere. She felt nervous about starting school next week and hoped Hailey would hold up to her promise of always being there no matter what, and even though she looked forward to seeing Isabelle before school started, she already knew that when her two best friends would call about partying, she'd have to tell them a lie.

And they called. And she lied. She had to babysit Christopher.

She wished she could have told them the truth. But tell them she wasn't into the partying thing anymore? Yeah, right. Maybe all she needed to say was how she didn't want to start her junior year the way her sophomore year had ended. That would have been the truth, just not the whole truth.

Chapter Nineteen

Zoe thanked her mom for the waffles and scrambled eggs; said "later" to Nicole, who had a mouth full of waffles, the syrup dripping down her chin; hugged Christopher, who wanted to know where she was going and could he come with her; then headed for the door for the first day of her junior year.

"Zoe," her mom said, "you look very cute, by the way."

She wasn't so sure that was the look she was going for when she dressed in her Moulin Rouge-inspired tank top, denim shorts, and black flip-flops. She had clipped her hair back with the vintage barrettes, leaving enough bangs to cover the scar. Her rhinestone bracelets dangled from her wrists, and she had painted her toenails and fingernails with Eggplant Sparkle polish. Dramatic was the word she was looking for. Did she need another mirror check?

"You look way hot," Nicole said, helping herself to another waffle. "Can I borrow your bracelets someday?"

Zoe gave them a twirl and smiled. "Absolutely."

At the high school parking lot, Zoe sat for a moment in

her car. She looked up at the two-story, red-brick structure with its towering center atrium. A purple-and-white banner read, Rock Ridge High, and below that, hung another banner, Welcome Students, Staff, and Teachers!

She decided that this year couldn't be any worse than her sophomore year, the beginning of which held nothing but nightmares for her—nightmares about not being able to find her classes, about the hallway stretching on forever, and just when she thought she had found her class, it disappeared and the hall stretched on forever again. Nightmares about forgetting her locker combination. But the worst nightmare was the one she had of sitting in the school cafeteria. Alone.

She headed toward the school, and before she knew it, she was in a swarm of students all heading toward the entrance. She took a deep breath and passed through the steel double doors just like everyone else.

First class: PE. A lousy way to start the day, and she knew it could only get better from there. PE may have been even easier had she brought her cane. But even with that, Ms. Herrmann probably wouldn't have shown much sympathy. Ms. Herrmann should have stayed in the military.

After PE, Zoe headed to her art class. She immediately spotted her friend Adam sitting toward the back. She slid into the seat next to him. He wore a black T-shirt, black jeans, black tennis shoes, and black wrist bands. Last year they had competed to see who could show up to school wearing the most black. He was a bit braver, sporting black hair ribbons. And when the kids teased him, his response was, "If they were good enough for our forefathers, they're good enough for me," and then he'd get on with life. She envied his ability to take everything in stride.

She hoped this year would be different, and that he'd stop wearing so much black. It was fun last year, but she thought it was old now. She was so done with looking like Wednesday Addams.

"Hey, Zoe, how was your summer?" Adam asked.

Had he not heard about the accident? Incident? Or whatever the hell it should be called?

"It was good," Zoe said, staring at his hair. "How was yours?"

"All good. My dad opened another art gallery farther west, and he let me display some of my paintings. I actually sold one."

"Really?"

"It was no biggie," Adam said. "I only made a couple hundred bucks, but I figured it's a start, anyway."

"That's great, Adam," she said, reaching into her portfolio and pulling out her sketch pad. She flipped to her warrior princess.

"That's good," Adam said, leaning toward her. "Damn, Zoe, you've really improved your shading technique since last year. And that is one hot warrior chick."

"Seriously? For real?"

"Yeah, hang-in-my-bedroom hot."

Zoe laughed and shook her head.

"Oh, and my hair." He tugged at the strand falling into his eyes. "Left the hair dye on a bit too long. I was actually going for a subtler shade of green."

Zoe giggled. "I know the feeling."

Mr. Martinez held up his hand to silence the class, and he opened the discussion to events or people or places that inspired and encouraged the art in the artist over the summer.

Unlike in other classes, the kids in art class actually raised their hands to talk about their art, their passion. One student talked about the vacation she took with her parents to the Grand Canyon and how the colors of the West inspired her to paint landscapes. Another talked about how photography helped him see the world from a different perspective, which helped him with sketching still lifes. Other students shared, but Zoe remained silent. How could she possibly tell them about the colors she had seen and felt in her near-death experience? They were so real. So vivid. Nothing like the colors here. So, she sat silent while everyone else shared, feeling frustrated, feeling like she wasn't a part of something.

Toward the end of the class, Mr. Martinez asked for volunteers to help with the fall art show, and yes, it wasn't until the end of October, but they had to plan now. Zoe looked around the room, then slowly raised her hand. She elbowed Adam. He slowly raised his. A few more hands.

Something to look forward to. Something to feel a part of. Back in the game.

Mr. Martinez thanked those who had raised their hands and then said, "You can enter two pieces, and they don't necessarily have to be anything that you've worked on in class. As soon as you know what you'd like to enter, let me know, and if you have any questions, don't hesitate to ask."

After art class, Zoe walked down the hall to her locker to grab her history book, and when the last number to her locker combination clicked into place, a familiar voice said, "You missed a great party Saturday night."

"Isabelle!"

Zoe spun around and gave Isabelle a big hug.

Isabelle said, "Last time I saw you, I didn't dare hug you this hard. Glad to know you're feeling better."

"I am. Thanks."

"Hailey was right."

"About what?"

"You really have changed."

Zoe wanted to tell her just how much, but instead said, "Sorry I didn't make it to your party."

"There's always next time," Isabelle said. "We have a lot of catching up to do."

Isabelle started right in on that catching up part as they walked down the hall to history. She told Zoe how she'd worked on Mozart's *Concerto in A Major* during band camp and how she couldn't wait to play it in the fall concert.

"Tryouts for orchestra seats are in two weeks," Isabelle said. "I really want first chair, but I guess I could live with second. But definitely not third."

And while Isabelle chatted on about camp, Zoe only partially heard her. How she wished she could tell her that the music she played, however beautiful, wasn't even close to what she had heard in that place like heaven, and she wondered if she'd ever be able to tell her.

History was boring, and not because the teacher spoke in a monotone. It was just boring, and Zoe counted down the minutes to lunch and thought the bell would never ring.

Isabelle, Hailey, and Zoe sat together for lunch at a window table and ate their pizza and talked about the latest girl/guy gossip and the new fall fashions and when they were going to go to the mall. Then Isabelle started talking about this guy she met in band camp, and when Hailey pushed for the details, Zoe tuned them out long enough to concentrate on her afternoon schedule. Biology followed lunch. She hoped that no incident would occur that would end in her regurgitating lunch, as it had last year when she sliced open a frog.

Last year, she and Adam had circulated a petition asking to abandon the practice of dissecting frogs, but with only a handful of signatures, the practice continued.

English, her least favorite, followed biology, and algebra, her most challenging, completed her day.

Zoe made it through biology and English, but about jumped out of her seat when Hailey walked into her algebra class.

"Last minute schedule change," Hailey whispered to her.

Zoe was feeling better about math already. Hailey got math, but that comfort turned into panic when she saw Vanessa Wellington saunter in and take her assigned seat right behind her.

Yeah, the universe really is on my side.

But not only did Zoe survive math class, even with Vanessa breathing on her neck, but before she knew it, she had also survived her first day of her junior year. Only a few kids asked about her limp, and no one asked about the scar. Hailey was right. It wasn't even noticeable under her bangs. And the only sign of the Gospel Girl Gang was Vanessa, who was actually much quieter than usual and who had acknowledged Zoe with nothing more than a tilt of her head and a sneer. And that breathing.

Zoe thought about the gang as she walked to her car after school. Vanessa, Tiffany, Claire, and Meagan. She remembered when she and Meagan were best friends back in middle school. But then Meagan got all cool in the ninth grade and ditched her. Her dad had received a huge promotion at the television station, and they moved to Whispering Willows, the side of town that came complete with a designer-label wardrobe and makeover.

But exit Meagan and enter Isabelle with her bright smile, belly laughs, frizzy red hair, myopic glasses, and a personality that most definitely made up for Meagan's. So why did Zoe still miss her sometimes?

Throughout the week, she occasionally saw Gabriel as they passed in the halls, and they acknowledged one another with nothing more than a quick smile and nod. On Friday, Gabriel took her aside and asked her if she and her friends would like to sit with him and his friends at lunch. Hailey and Isabelle thought he was hot, and later, asked Zoe if he was the new guy in her life. She told them he wasn't, then wondered how they could have looked so disappointed and shocked and skeptical all at the same time. She laughed. "Just friends," she had said, "so please, spare us both any rumors."

Zoe decided her junior year was going to be different, but different in a good way. A very good way. It didn't take her long to realize how wrong she was.

Chapter Twenty

"There she is. She's gotten so weird," Vanessa said, pointing her fry toward the entrance of the cafeteria. "Off-the-charts weird."

Tiffany, Claire, and Meagan stopped munching on their fries and looked up.

"That's Zoe Weber," Tiffany said, nonchalantly. "What's so weird about her?"

"That's Zoe?" Meagan said, wide-eyed. "My god, she looks so different."

"Zoe's doing community service at the hospital," Vanessa said.

"So what's so weird about that?" Tiffany asked.

"Tiff, you don't know anything," Vanessa said. "Listen."

And it was the way she said "listen" that the three of them leaned in, because the three of them knew that everything Vanessa said was gospel—not to be confused with gossip, which was something all the other girls did.

"Some totally weird things have been happening at the hospital since she's been there," Vanessa said.

"Oh, my god, like drugs missing?" Claire asked.

"She's stealing drugs?" asked Meagan.

Tiffany dropped her fry. "Drugs? If she's stealing drugs, I'm in."

"Not drugs, you idiots," Vanessa said.

"Then what? What's she stealing?" Meagan asked.

"She's not stealing anything," Vanessa said. "If you'd shut up for a minute, I'd tell you."

They leaned in even closer.

"Okay, girls, assume your position," Vanessa said.

Assume your position meant they were to stop acting as though they were about to hear the juiciest story ever, and instead act sophisticated—in order to give off such an air, one must never appear to be in gossip mode. So, they leaned back, and with an air of nonchalance, asked Vanessa what she knew for sure.

Vanessa took a long sip of her soda through the straw, the only way she would drink liquids, so as never to smudge her lipstick. "Like people getting better. People that never stood a chance. People who were really, really, and I mean really, sick are like whah-lah, up and out of there. My mom's friend works at the hospital, and she said she's never seen anything like it. Strange, huh?" She took another long sip of her soda.

"Well, yeah, that's strange," Meagan said, "but what makes them think Zoe has anything to do with that?"

"Meagan," Vanessa said, "why do you always have to be such a devil's advocate?"

"What's a devil's advocate?" Claire asked.

Meagan pulled a notebook and a pen from her backpack. "I think I'm sensing a story here for the school paper."

Claire looked at her. "You're going to write a story about devils?"

Meagan looked at her. "No, you idiot, I'm—"

"Who's that guy that just walked up to her?" Tiffany said. "He's hot."

Vanessa turned to look. "What is someone that hot doing talking to Zoe Weber?" she asked.

"Yeah, he is kind of hot," said Meagan. "But Zoe's not looking too bad herself, actually."

"Get real, Meagan," said Vanessa. "She's a loser, and I'm going to find out what that loser is doing with that guy."

"You're not," said Meagan.

"Watch me," said Vanessa. She waited patiently, and at just the right moment, stood, turned, and bumped smack into Gabriel, spilling her soda down the front of his form-fitting white henley.

She looked up at him. "Oh, I'm so sorry. I guess I should look where I'm going." She brushed the bubbles from his shirt, her fingers lingering on his chest.

The girls giggled.

"No worries," Gabriel said. "Accidents happen."

"No, they don't," Zoe said.

Claire handed Vanessa a napkin.

Vanessa dabbed Gabriel's shirt with the napkin, soaking up the drops of soda. "There. That's better."

Zoe looked at Gabriel. *He's mesmerized. He's totally mesmerized by her.* She looked back at Vanessa. How she wanted to reach up and punch her, a good one right across that dainty little jaw, or maybe a swift one to that delicate nose of hers. One good swing would be all it would take. If she could reach. Why must she always feel so defeated?

Zoe grabbed Gabriel by the arm and led him to the cafeteria line.

"What the hell was that all about?" she asked, taking a tray.

"What was what all about?" Gabriel asked, taking a tray for himself.

"I saw how you were looking at her. Yeah, she's pretty. And smart, which really sucks. Pretty, smart, and mean. Can't get a better combination than that." Zoe reached for a slice of pizza and threw it down on her plate. "But I guess that doesn't matter with you guys."

He burst out laughing.

"You find that funny?" she asked.

He reached for a fruit bowl. "I wasn't looking at her because I thought she was hot."

"It sure looked like it to me."

A student yelled, "Hey, keep the line moving!"

A cafeteria worker echoed the student's demand. "You two need to stop talking and start moving."

Zoe looked up at the woman and wanted to tell her to get an attitude adjustment already, but muttered a sorry instead. She threw fries onto her plate, grabbed a handful of napkins and ketchup packets, and walked toward the far corner of the cafeteria.

Gabriel sat opposite her. "So," he said, "are you ready to listen to what I have to say?"

Zoe, about to take a bite of her pizza, nodded.

He leaned forward and whispered, "I was looking at her aura."

She dropped her pizza. "Her what?"

"Her aura, her energy field," he said.

"I know what it is," she said. "Seriously?"

"It's kind of freaky sometimes, but yeah, that's my thing since my NDE."

"So, what did you see?" she asked, slowly, not too sure she really wanted to know.

He leaned over the table and whispered, "She has this incredibly dark, misty, oozy kind of aura, which tells me that she likes to sneak out in the middle of the night wearing only a black hooded robe. She goes deep into the forest and howls at the moon. Sometimes she even moons the moon, but only if it's full, otherwise she'll bring bad luck to herself and to her friends."

Zoe sat there and just looked at him.

"What?" he asked.

She burst out laughing and tossed a fry at him. "You are so full of shit."

He leaned back and grinned. "Yeah, but I had you going."

"You did not have me going."

"Yeah, I did. I had you going."

She smiled and shook her head. She ate a few fries. "So, you're not going to tell me what you really saw?"

He reached over and took one of her fries and swirled it in the ketchup. "She's no more troubled than any of us," he said, popping the fry into his mouth. "Maybe just a bit more insecure than most."

"That's it?"

"You liked my other answer better."

"I did."

She grew silent.

"What is it?" he asked. "What's bothering you now?"

"Just thinking." She poked at a mushroom. "Thinking about how I never thought a guy like you would ever want to hang out with a girl like me."

He looked down. "A couple of years ago, I probably wouldn't have." He sighed heavily. "Back then, my ego was getting in the way of a lot of things, including happiness."

She thought about that word, ego. It can do that sometimes. Sneak up and steal happiness.

"You never did tell me," she said.

"Tell you what?"

"About your NDE."

A sudden stillness swept over them, and why did she feel like she'd touched something she shouldn't have?

"It wasn't that hot," he said.

"But that's a good thing, right?" she said.

He chuckled. "Well, not being hot there probably would be a good thing, but I didn't mean it that way."

Zoe wondered what he did mean, but she figured she'd already asked enough questions. Besides, how could she possibly expect him to tell her about his NDE when she hadn't even told her friends about her own?

Chapter Twenty-one

"So, you ready?" Hailey asked as she and Zoe walked into algebra.

"I am so not ready," Zoe said.

"Seriously, we're barely into the school year," Hailey said. "I can't believe that Mr. Sumner is already giving us a test."

Zoe rolled her eyes. "Seriously," she said, walking toward her seat.

"Hey, Zoe," Clyde said.

"Hey, Clyde, how's it going?"

"It's going. Good luck on the test."

She liked Clyde even if he was a little on the nerdy side and so serious all the time. She rarely saw him laugh or even smile. She took her seat behind him and flipped her textbook open one last time before the test. She scanned through a few pages. Flipped a few pages, scanned some more.

"Like that's really going to help," Vanessa said.

Zoe looked up at Vanessa, annoyed at the interruption, then almost burst out laughing at the thought of her mooning the moon.

"Something funny, Web?"

She shook her head.

"Better not be," Vanessa said, taking her seat behind Zoe.

Mr. Sumner held up his hands to silence the class. "Take your seats. Take your seats, quickly. We need to get started."

Mr. Sumner handed out the test, reminding the students that even though this was the first test of the semester, it was crucial for their overall performance. Clyde handed Zoe the test, and she passed one to Vanessa.

Zoe began.

Name in the upper right hand corner.

Okay, first question. That's the first question? My god, that's an easy one.

She scribbled in the answer and moved on. Got that one too. She went down the line of questions, finished the first page, then flipped to the second page. About halfway down the second page, she paused a moment to glance around the room. It didn't appear as though anyone else was on the second page. They all looked like zombies, just staring at the pages, their pencils moving slowly. She completed the second page and went on to the third and final page. Her mind moved faster than she could write.

What kind of test is this? What got into Mr. Sumner?

She put her pencil down, sat back, and glanced around the room again. Pencils tapping on the desk, pencils tapping against the lips, legs bouncing ever so slightly, legs bouncing with nervous energy, deep sighs, a pencil dropped to the floor, erasing, eraser waste brushed to the floor, rewriting, erasing again, coughing, someone coughing, someone else coughing.

Is coughing contagious? Zoe knew that sometimes a cough came from nervousness. *What's there to be nervous about? The test was easy. The easiest ever.*

The room seemed engulfed in eraser dust.

Even Hailey seems to be struggling.

Maybe a page was missing. She inconspicuously looked across the aisle at another student's test pages. *Looks like three pages. Yep, three.*

She sighed, looked over her test again, and decided she was indeed done. As she made her way toward Mr. Sumner's desk, she felt the eyes of the students on her, and why did it feel so creepy? She exchanged a quick glance with Hailey, detecting an odd look from her before she went back to her test, erasing something.

She felt as though she was moving in slow motion. Finally, she stood in front of Mr. Sumner's desk. She waited for him to look up, but his nose was buried deep within the pages of a book.

"Mr. Sumner."

He lowered his book and peered up at her. "Do you have a question, Zoe?"

"No sir. I've finished."

He removed his reading glasses, leaned his forearms on his desk, and clasped his hands. "Zoe, a lot is riding on this test." He glanced at his watch. "You still have about fifteen minutes. I suggest that you use them."

"No, Mr. Sumner, I've finished." She laid the test down on his desk.

"Are you sure you don't want to check everything over?"

"I'm sure."

She turned around to go back to her seat, but bumped into Clyde. They excused one another, and what was that look he gave her? A look of sympathy? Pity?

She slid into her seat, then pulled her sketch pad from her portfolio. She looked at her warrior with her long dark tresses and intense dark eyes. Dressed in full armor, sword held high, she was poised to lead her comrades into battle against the enemy. She thought Adam was right. Her warrior did look seductive and fierce and quite capable of bringing down the enemy. She was about to start shading the towers of the enemy fortress when she felt breathing on the back of her neck.

"So," Vanessa whispered in her saccharin voice. "Too hard for you, Web? Couldn't finish? Gave up?"

Without turning around, Zoe whispered back, "I finished it."

"Liar."

"I'll bet I scored higher than you."

"You've never scored higher than me on anything."

Mr. Sumner looked up from his reading. "Do I hear talking? No talking please."

Zoe glanced up at Mr. Sumner. His nose was already back in his book.

"Bet's on," Vanessa said. "Name it."

"No, you name it," Zoe said. "Bet away. Whatever you want."

"That's brave, not to mention stupid, but I would expect no less from you," Vanessa said. "The bet is this. You have to wash my BMW every day for a week inside and out, and it better look good and smell good when you're done, and none of that vanilla or pine smell crap in there either. Got that?"

"I do, but I don't know, Vanessa. I was thinking of something a little more high profile."

"Like what?"

"Like serving whomever wins lunch for a week."

"You're on, loser."

Mr. Sumner looked up from his book again. "Do I hear talking? I said no talking."

Zoe moved her hand behind her and felt Vanessa's hand wrap around hers, giving it a firm squeeze.

***

"I didn't cheat!" Zoe said.

She sat in an office she hadn't sat in since that time she got busted for smoking pot in the boys' bathroom. With Adam. They had both underestimated Ms. Herrmann's ability to sniff out trouble. The office didn't look much different, other than a more recent family picture on the corner of Principal Huxley's desk with a new grandchild.

Dr. Huxley thumbed through a thick folder, then stopped and looked up at her. "Zoe, we have reason to believe you did."

"Do you have actual proof?" her mom asked.

"I got this, Mom," said Zoe.

Zoe proceeded to explain to Dr. Huxley how she and her friend, Gabriel, have been studying together, how he'd been helping her, drilling her repetitively and relentlessly and mercilessly, almost to the point of needing an aspirin and a nap.

Her mom looked at her. "Gabriel? Who's Gabriel?"

"My tutor," Zoe answered.

"I didn't know you had a tutor," Mom said. She looked at Dr. Huxley. "I didn't know she had a tutor."

Dr. Huxley continued, "Tutor or no tutor, I have someone who said she saw you cheating."

"She?" Zoe asked. "That she wouldn't be Vanessa Wellington, would it?"

"And you would need to know that why?" asked Dr. Huxley.

"Because we placed a bet," Zoe said. "She lost. Of course she's going to say I cheated."

"Zoe," Mom said, "you tell me you have a tutor and now you tell me you place bets on tests? You don't make a game of grades by placing bets."

Dr. Huxley impatiently tapped his pen on his desk. "Zoe, were you or were you not looking across the aisle at another student's test?"

"No! I mean, yes, I looked to make sure the test was only three pages long, not to see someone else's answers."

"What?" her mom asked.

"I didn't cheat," Zoe said, softy.

Her mom stood. "Dr. Huxley, unless you have absolute proof, and not hearsay, then I believe this meeting is over."

Dr. Huxley flipped through the folder again, leaned back, and sighed. "I don't understand how any student who's pulling Cs and Ds can all of a sudden score an A."

Zoe leaned toward his desk and was about to say

something, but felt the gentle touch of her mom's arm on hers, pulling her back.

"Are we done here?" her mom asked.

"We're done, Mrs. Weber, Zoe," Dr. Huxley said, closing the folder.

Once outside the school, Zoe said, "You totally rocked in there, Mom. Thanks."

"I'm proud of you, Zoe," her mom said, reaching into her purse for her sunglasses. "And tell your friend that he's welcome to our home for dinner anytime."

Zoe smiled. "I will."

Her mom reached for the door to her SUV. "Zoe?"

She looked at her mom. What was that look? Doubt layered in confusion?

"Never mind," her mom said, climbing into the SUV.

Zoe breathed a sigh of relief, and while climbing in, thought she heard her mom mumble something under her breath about that A.

When Zoe got home, she ran into the sanctuary of her bedroom and plopped down on her bed. She worked on her drawing, sketching the background fortress and towers. She was trying to come up with a flag design for the towers, but couldn't think of one. Her mind was preoccupied with that math test. How had she done it?

Memories slowly filtered in from last year's math class, which she had almost failed, but the kind words of her math teacher, Mrs. Fleming, had kept her going. Zoe thought that she was perhaps the most patient teacher in the school, if not the world.

"Someday," Mrs. Fleming had said, "you'll get it. Someday, you'll plop right down and it will all fall into place. Be persistent. Be relentless. Be patient."

She remembered Mrs. Fleming saying not only that, but also how students sometimes gave up too early. "They've convinced themselves they're no good," she had said. "One more step and they might have had it." And something about creating one's own self-fulfilling prophecy.

Was that what had happened during the math test? The pieces magically fell into place like Mrs. Fleming said they would?

She thought back to her near-death experience and all those scrolls and how she had been sucked into them, absorbing all the information contained within.

Is that how I did it? Am I some kind of freak now? Mentally able to regurgitate whatever it is I need to, whenever I need to know it?

She didn't know what to think, what to believe. She wanted, needed, to talk with someone. And she would. Tonight. At the meeting.

Chapter Twenty-Two

Zoe walked into the counseling room and gave a friend-
ly, yet hurried, hello to Melissa and Jamie and Stephen
and Emily and all the others while glancing around, looking for Gabriel.

She spotted Michael over by the refreshment table,
munching on a cookie, and walked over to him. "Hey,
Michael, have you seen Gabriel?"

He brushed a crumb from his mouth. "You like him,
don't you. Are you in love with him or something?"

"Or something," she said.

"Well, he is a nice guy even if he does call me Squirt.
Don't you think?"

"Yeah, he's a nice guy."

"All the girls like Gabriel. Do you like Gabriel?"

"Yes," she said, with a bit of an unintentional hiss on the
s. She took a breath. "I like him already, he's a great guy. So,
have you seen him?"

"Yeah."

"Well, then, Michael," she said. "Where is he?"

"Right behind you."

Zoe's eyes widened, then narrowed.

Michael grinned, turned, and walked away.

"Looking for me?" Gabriel asked.

She slowly turned around. "Ah, yeah. We need to talk. Privately."

"Zoe, this is group. We can't talk privately. Whatever you have to say to me should be spoken to the whole group."

"I'm not ready to share this. Not yet." She looked at Gabriel with pleading eyes, and it took her only a few seconds of gauging his reaction before she said, "Never mind," and walked away.

She plopped down on the sofa, and soon after, Gabriel plopped down next to her.

Fine. Sit next to me. But it's not going to make me feel any better.

Joanna began the meeting. Zoe didn't care. Her inner turmoil over that math test occupied her, and she didn't hear a word Joanna or anyone else said. Scoring almost perfect thrilled her, but how could she explain to anyone how she had managed an impossible feat when she didn't understand it herself. Would she be able to do it again, or was it a fluke? Did she even want to do that again?

Oh, but how many times had she wanted to beat Vanessa at something, anything. That damn Vanessa. That smart, rich bitch. And now she had, finally. So why, instead of feeling smug, was she feeling miserable?

Zoe heard her name. Everyone was looking at her, waiting for her to say something. She heard Joanna's soft voice.

"Do you have anything you'd like to share?"

"Ah, no, I'm good." And in her spoken words, she tried to squish her real thoughts, her real desire, but the thoughts raced anyway. She should say something, shouldn't she? No, she decided, not tonight. Not when she felt this way.

Joanna stood up. "Well, everyone, that was a great session."

"Actually," Zoe said, "I do have a question."

Joanna sat back down. Zoe felt all eyes in the room on her again, but not like when she walked to Mr. Sumner's desk, her math test in hand. Not those eyes. Those eyes were judging, almost mocking. These eyes were kind and full of love and concern and compassion.

"Well," Zoe said, "I was just wondering, I mean, here I am with all of you who have something, a gift, or whatever it is you call it, and I was wondering how soon after your NDE did you realize you even had something like that?"

"That's an excellent question, Zoe," Joanna said. "Anyone want to share?"

And as soon as Joanna asked the question, the kids couldn't answer fast enough. Right away, one said. A few months, said another. A matter of days, said yet another. So unexpectedly. A flash, an instant, and their lives had been changed forever. No going back to their old life, no matter how much they wished they could. They were now healers, mentalists, mediums, but never manipulators, energy drainers, healer-stealers, or a stealer of anyone's energy or gift.

My god, Zoe thought, *people actually can do that? Steal the gift? Steal the energy?*

And why was it that every time she asked one question, a hundred more seemed to surface?

"Zoe," Joanna said, "just because you haven't received a gift doesn't mean you're not going to. We're all different. A gift may come, and it may not, but either way, please understand, you're always welcome here." Joanna glanced at her watch. "Well, we've run out of time. Another great session. Do I have volunteers for cleanup?"

Gabriel raised his hand, and with his other, grabbed Zoe's and raised her hand high into the air. "Zoe and I volunteer," he said.

She shot him a look. "We do?"

He smiled and nodded.

"Thank you, Zoe and Gabriel," Joanna said. "The door will lock behind you. See you next week."

After everyone had left, Gabriel walked over to the refreshment table and tossed his empty bottle of water into the recycling bin.

"Want one?" he asked, holding up two more bottles.

Zoe pulled her knees up to her chest and shook her head.

He put one back and unscrewed the cap to his and took a sip. "So, is that what's bothering you? You don't have a gift and you have to sit here and listen to everyone else talk about theirs? Feeling left out?"

She didn't know how to start, not sure if she even wanted to. She had one simple question to ask him before the meeting, but now she had enough to keep him there all night. What were these kids? The idea of time travel didn't seem so weird now after all.

"Hey, Zoe, I know this is confusing."

She looked at him, an almost hopeless look. "Right when I'm beginning to feel comfortable here, someone says something, or something happens in my life to turn it all upside down again."

He walked back over to her and took a seat on the armrest of the sofa. "It'll get easier, I promise." He took another sip. "But it's not going to get easier unless you talk."

She took a deep breath. "I told my mom a really big lie today."

He chuckled. "Don't we all at times lie to our parents?"

"But this one involved you."

A shift.

A pause.

She pushed a strand of hair away from her face. "I told her that you helped me study for a math test."

"You told her what?"

"I'm sorry, Gabriel. I didn't know what else to say. I had to come up with something."

"I don't get it."

She stood up, walked over to the refreshment table, grabbed that bottle of water, and just stood there, staring at the bottle.

"I'm listening," he said.

"I totally nailed that math test," she said. "The highest score."

"Zoe, that's great."

"But I kind of cheated."

"Okay, none of this is making any sense."

She looked at him. "I passed that math test because in my NDE my grandma took me to this place where there were hundreds, no thousands of scrolls. I think it was called something like the Hall of Records."

"I've heard of that," he said.

"You have?"

"No."

"Gabriel, I'm being serious."

"Sorry. Go ahead. I'll shut up."

So, Gabriel remained quiet while Zoe told him what had happened when she was in the Hall of Records, and how she was actually in the math scrolls, absorbing and processing all of it.

He walked over to her. "And so you think you retained all that information?"

She nodded. "So, I guess I do have a gift, but now that I have one, I'm not so sure I even want it."

He ran his fingers through his hair and softly chuckled. "Isn't that the way it is? You think you want it, and then when you do get it, you don't want it."

She forced a smile. "That's not all."

"Still listening," he said.

She went on to explain the bet with Vanessa. "I feel kind of guilty about all of it," she said.

"This is all new for you," he said. "Don't be so hard on yourself."

She stood there for a moment, feeling the space between them, a gap, a small gap that seemed to gently close in and hug them, warmly. An energy. A nice, warm energy flowing through her, and she knew from looking into Gabriel's eyes that he felt it too.

"Come on," he said. "Let's get this place cleaned up."

She grabbed the cleaning wipes and pulled one out. "You never told me," she said, wiping down the buffet table.

"Told you what?"

She stopped and looked at him. "How you ended up coming here. About your near-death experience."

"Drowning accident."

"Accident?"

"Incident, I mean. Family vacation at St. Thomas last Christmas. The current got the best of me."

"You seem too strong, too athletic."

"Even the best of us can get sucked under." He pulled the trash bag from the wastebasket and tied it. "God, it was so beautiful."

Zoe's eyes brightened, her face lit up. "Your near-death experience?"

"No. St. Thomas."

"Gabriel!"

He laughed, and she shook her head, but soon found herself laughing right along with him.

"Zoe?"

She grew still and nervous at the sudden change in his demeanor.

So quiet.

So contemplative.

"Yeah?"

He leaned up against the buffet table. "I used to get upset

whenever my plans got interrupted, but now I think that whenever life interrupts, it's a chance for me to slow down and think about what's important. Interruptions seem to do that. Force us to pause and think. Sometimes the interruption can be tragic, but I've learned that if you can let go of the appearance, let go of what you think you're perceiving, then perhaps instead of seeing something tragic, you'll see something like magic, and maybe that's why life interrupted us to begin with."

The words *tragic* and *magic* and *interruption* played on her mind like delicate musical notes. Tragic. Maybe her car accident wasn't. Interruptions. She hated them. She didn't have time to pause and think. Maybe she should start.

She looked at him and smiled. "So, what you're saying is, is that when life interrupts, that's God's way of giving you a good, swift kick in the ass?"

He laughed. "Yeah, I guess so."

The word *magic* continued to linger in her mind long after they'd cleaned up and walked out the door. That's the word she had remembered hearing when people talked about her grandma. People had come from all over the country to see her, all those people whose health had supposedly improved after being with her. And how was that possible if it wasn't magic?

Twenty-Three

Vanessa slammed the lunch tray down so hard the pizza slice bounced, and the apple bounced too, right onto the floor.

"You don't have to be such a sore loser," Hailey said, retrieving the rolling apple.

"I don't know how you did what you did, Zoe Weber," Vanessa said. "But I intend to find out."

Isabelle raised her hands in the air. "Oooh, and I'll huff and I'll puff and I'll blow your house down."

"Yeah," said Hailey, handing the apple to Zoe, "and over the river and through the woods."

And something about Vanessa going into the woods got Zoe all giggly, and before she knew it, she and Hailey and Isabelle were holding their stomachs in raucous laughter.

Vanessa huffed, and holding her head high, walked toward her own table and snapped her fingers. Tiffany, Claire, and Meagan jumped up and followed her out of the cafeteria.

After they had left, Zoe wiped away her tears of laughter

and looked at the apple. She rolled it around in her fingers. "It appears to be a bit bruised."

"Like Vanessa's ego," Hailey said.

The girls burst into laughter again, and their laughter turned to giggles, then faded into silence. A haunting feeling of guilt had come over Zoe, a guilt she couldn't shake. She felt perhaps if she spared Vanessa from further humiliation, however deserved and however long overdue, then perhaps, just perhaps, she might somehow feel less guilty. So, in that one day, as far as Zoe was concerned, the bet had been fulfilled.

Hailey stuffed fries into her mouth. "Zoe, how did you do it?"

Another lie was forming, and Zoe wondered what a lie would look like, be like, if a person held it in their hands. Would it look like scum floating on the surface of a pond, smell like dirty rags, feel like a steel wool pad brushing against delicate skin, taste like sour milk, sound like a freight train?

Zoe wiped sauce from the corner of her mouth. "Well, if it wasn't for Gabriel tutoring me, I never could have done it."

"Gabriel?" Hailey asked. "And that's it?"

Zoe nodded and took another bite of her pizza, but looked up at them and saw the doubt in their eyes. Why couldn't she bring herself to tell her two best friends what was really going on in her life? How she'd really met Gabriel. The meetings, and the kids, and how awesome they all were. Visiting Grandma in heaven. The scrolls. The music, how magnificent. And the fairies, how exquisite.

But wait. She did try, didn't she? That day in her bedroom? That first day she came home from the hospital. She did try to tell them, just as she had tried to tell her family. It was the drugs, she had heard. It was a dream. You need to rest. Should she try telling them again?

"So, Zoe, do you think you'll be able to go tonight?" Hailey asked.

"Go where?" Zoe asked.

"Where have you been for the last five minutes?" Isabelle asked. "To the movies with us."

"It's Wednesday. I have my counseling, I mean, Christopher, I have to babysit Christopher," Zoe said, wondering why her words had jumped ahead of her brain just now.

"Why can't your sister babysit him?" Hailey asked.

"Because her degree in nursing is more important than my social life," Zoe said.

"Why does she even live at home if she's in college?" Isabelle asked. "I mean, college parties are awesome, or so I've heard."

"She's not into the partying thing," Zoe said.

"Are you sure you're even sisters?" Isabelle asked.

"I'm sure."

***

Zoe looked in her rearview mirror, and what she saw set her heart palpitating. What to do? Where to go? She jumped at the buzz of her cell phone.

"Aren't you coming tonight?" Gabriel asked.

"Gabriel, I'm on my way, but Vanessa is following me."

"Okay, let me think."

A pause.

A really long pause.

"Gabriel, you still with me?" she asked.

"I got it," he said. "Drive to the library."

"The library?"

"Five blocks south of the center. Two-story glass-and-brick building, clock tower, right side."

"But what about the meeting?"

"I'll see you at the library," he said.

A few minutes later, she spotted the clock tower and pulled into the lot, parking close to the front entry doors. She glanced in her rearview mirror. Vanessa was slowly pulling in, but then braked. Zoe wondered if perhaps she'd changed her mind, but then she eased into a parking spot just inside the lot entrance.

Zoe hurried into the library, and once inside, stood awestruck in the atrium. Exotic palms with bold leaves and spiky foliage graced both sides of the entryway. The fading light of the sun filtered through the massive windows and skylights, casting a golden glow that seemed to breathe energy into the wood-and-glass structure. The soft voice of Gabriel calling her brought her out of her spell. She hustled over and slid into a seat across from him. He held up a book on algebra, and one on memory and concentration.

"Nice," she said, grinning.

He glanced over her shoulder. "Don't turn around, but here she comes, and she's not alone."

He started rambling off math equations and she

answered them. She surprised herself at how readily she knew the answers. She thought that this was going to be a game of pretend. He would pretend to ask and she would pretend to answer, but every question he asked, she knew. She was actually beginning to feel a bit uncomfortable, but at the same time, she liked how it made her feel.

She told him to slow down. She was starting to feel like a freak. He stopped and looked up from his book. But this time when he looked up, he wasn't looking at her.

"So, it's the library that's become your new hangout," Vanessa said. "I never would have thought."

"Likewise, Vanessa," Zoe said. "So, what are you doing here?"

"Studying," she answered. "Isn't that right, girls?"

Tiffany, Claire, and Meagan nodded.

Like puppets.

"You can join us if you like," Gabriel said. "We're just going over some math problems."

Vanessa positioned her hands on the edge of the table and leaned toward him. "There's a lot of things I'd like to join you in Gabriel, but math isn't one of them." She turned to Zoe. "So that's it. Zoe plus tutor equals ace a math test? That kind of equation doesn't add up."

"Gabriel's a good tutor," Zoe said.

"I'm sure that's not all he's good at," Vanessa said, straightening up.

Her entourage giggled.

Vanessa continued, "Just one more thing I'd like to clear up."

"Yeah, what's that?" Zoe asked.

"How is it that an internal investigation at St. Francis Hospital involves you?" Vanessa asked.

An internal investigation? Zoe wondered. *Is that why those two men are there? But why would it involve me?*

"You didn't even know, did you?" Vanessa said.

Zoe shifted in her seat. "Whatever investigation is going on at the hospital has nothing to do with me," she said. "Besides, it's really none of your business."

Vanessa rested her palms on the edge of the table again and leaned into Zoe. "I'm not through with you yet, Weber," she said, stretching out the *r*, and Zoe thought Vanessa sounded like a growling tiger, and she was the prey.

"Come on, girls," Vanessa said, snapping her fingers. "Let's get out of here and leave these two to their books."

The clicking of their shoes became fainter. Zoe shifted in her seat, staring at the book on memory and concentration.

Gabriel gently tapped his finger on the book. "They're gone now, Zoe."

She let out a heavy sigh and rubbed her temples. "I'm beginning to think that there's something more to my NDE." She looked up at him. "I mean, it's bad enough that I've become a math whiz, but maybe there is something more going on with me."

"Zoe, take your time with all this," he said. "We can still go to the meeting tonight, or we can hang out here."

Silence.

"Zoe, you still with me?"

"I'm tired of lying. I've lied to my mom about how I aced

the math test, I lied to my mom and Charles about what the meetings are all about, and I haven't even told my friends the truth of how we met."

Gabriel sat silent for awhile, his fingers tapping on the table as though drumming up an old memory.

"That's irritating, Gabriel."

He stopped.

"Zoe, Kurt Vonnegut wrote this book."

"I know, *Slaughterhouse-Five*, and no, I didn't read it."

"No, not that book."

"He didn't write that? I though he wrote that."

Gabriel waved his hand as though growing impatient with her. "No, Zoe, I didn't mean that one. Yes, he wrote that book, but I'm talking about another book he wrote. *A Man without a Country*. In it, he says that when he dies, he would like to go to heaven to ask somebody, 'What's the good news and what's the bad news?'"

"That sounds like a good idea," Zoe said. "I'd like to ask, 'What the hell was that all about?'" She chuckled.

"Zoe?"

He's serious again.

"Yeah?"

"I think I'd leave out the word *hell*."

"Well, let's hope God has a sense of humor," she said, "because if not, then we'll all be going there."

"It's a nice thought," he said, "that God would have a sense of humor, I mean." He paused. "Zoe, we don't know what the good news is and what the bad news is because we don't know what the truth is. We have so many people telling us what to believe, and after hearing the same thing over and over and over again, it becomes our truth. But what is your truth? Do you even know what is true for you?"

She shrugged.

"Zoe, the truth about what's going on with you will be revealed in its own time."

"And the truth shall set you free!" Zoe said, waving her arms in the air like a zealous preacher. "Yippee."

He laughed.

"Come on," she said, standing up. "Let's get out of here."

"Do you want to go to the meeting?" he asked.

She nodded.

Once at the meeting, they apologized to the group and to Joanna for being late. Zoe plopped down on a meditation pillow next to the sofa. Gabriel sat on the arm of the sofa next to Michael, who munched on an oatmeal raisin cookie. Melissa and Jamie were there, as well as Stephen and Emily, who held Faith, which seemed to comfort her like cookies comforted Michael.

Zoe listened as Joanna continued talking about relationships and how they can change, and not always for the better, after a person has had a near-death experience.

Relationships. Zoe found them to be difficult with the NDE and without the NDE. How can anybody win? Thoughts of Dylan crept in, and as hard as she tried to dismiss him—his touch, his humor, his laugh—thoughts of him kept invading.

Joanna then moved on to the topic of being open to whatever shows up in life, and she talked a bit on forgiveness, both familiar topics in these sessions. Zoe wondered if she could ever forgive Dylan for being such a jerk. Then, she felt Gabriel gently nudge her. He pointed to the doorway.

Dylan?

She looked at Gabriel and then back toward the door. He was gone. Then she wondered if she had even seen him at all. She looked at Gabriel as if to say, *I didn't tell him I was here. I haven't told anyone*, but with the soft look in his eyes, she realized that she didn't need to.

She excused herself from the group and stepped out into the hallway. *Where did he go?* She walked toward the front door and wondered if he'd left and had simply come just to check things out.

She stepped outside into the cool air and to the chirping of crickets. A cigarette butt flew out from behind a Jeep. And why, as she approached him, did she feel as though butterflies were fluttering and bees were swarming all over inside of her?

Dylan was leaning against the spare tire, hands stuffed into his jean pockets.

"I suppose you're wondering how I knew you were here," he said, but before she could say anything, he abruptly straightened up, then swayed back. He quickly grabbed hold of the spare tire. "Your aunt told me."

"My aunt told you?"

He nodded. "I went to the hospital hoping that after you got out of school you'd be there. I was directed to your aunt's office, and after she realized who I was . . . damn, that woman really laid into me. She's tough."

"Yep, that's my aunt," Zoe said.

"She told me some stuff, stuff she probably shouldn't have." He kicked at something. "So, is it true?"

Zoe eyed him suspiciously.

"You actually died that day?" he asked.

"Yeah," she said, the word barely audible.

"I'm sorry. I am so sorry."

His eyes moistened and his body trembled. She wanted to grab him and hold him. She wanted to tell him that everything was all right. But she couldn't.

He told her how he had to beg her aunt to tell him where she was.

"And so here I am," he said.

"You went to the hospital to apologize?" Zoe asked. "It sounds like you really didn't even know what you were apologizing for."

He nodded. "I went to apologize for upsetting you that day in the bookstore, and now I'm apologizing not only for that, but for not believing you when you tried to tell me about your near-death experience, and for being such an ass."

"That you were."

"Here," he said, brushing past her and reaching into his Jeep. "You forgot these."

He handed her the two books.

Zoe took the books from him and stared at them for a few moments. "Thank you," she said.

He brushed his finger across her arm. "Zoe, I do care about you."

She continued to look at the books.

"You don't believe me?" he asked.

"I'm not sure what to believe right now."

"I've missed you," he said. "I've missed us."

Did he just say "us"?

And she liked the sound of that word. Us.

"Then, tell me," she said, looking up at him.

"Tell you what?"

"Tell me how wonderful I am."

"What?"

"You heard me. Tell me how wonderful I am."

"Okay, you're wonderful."

"Hmm, not good enough."

"Okay, you're wonderful and caring."

"Keep going."

"Okay," he said. "You're beautiful, witty, fun, and the most wonderful, incredible woman I've ever known, and I can't comprehend living my life without you in it."

"Warming up, I see."

"In more ways than one." He wrapped his hands around the back of her neck. "How's this to prove it to you?"

Zoe felt his strong body press into hers, his mouth moist on hers, her body growing warm.

Soft.

Passionate.

Slow.

Kisses.

Safe and secure in his embrace.

Just like she used to feel.

Loved him.
Loved this moment.
Loved her life again.

Twenty-Four

Zoe stood in the doorway of the art room. This was it. She looked at the kids knowing that she would probably never see any of them again. She thought how brave they were and how they had taught her more than she had taught them. So much more. It almost made her cry at the thought of having to say good-bye to Nathan and Nina and Tim and Hannah and all the others.

She walked up to Tim, and just as she was about to tell him that it was her last day and that she wished him the best, he stopped painting the black spots on his dairy cow and looked up at her. "Hi, Zoe." And then, "How do you do that thing with your hands?"

Whatever teary-eyed emotion she was about to unload became bottled up in a layer of confusion instead. "What thing?" she asked.

"Your hands change color like when I mix paint," he said. "I saw them. A couple of weeks ago when you had your hand on Hannah's back. First yellow, then gold, then purple." He dipped his paintbrush back into the black paint.

"It was way cool."

What was he talking about? She stared at him, not too long, but long enough to contemplate how sickly he was now. How does she tell a child who's dying of cancer that he's hallucinating? Her training didn't teach her how to handle that one.

He looked up at her. "It's okay. You don't have to tell me."

Zoe couldn't bear to tell him that he must have been seeing things. She shrugged it off. "Tim, where's Hannah?"

She looked forward to seeing Hannah's seascapes. No large whitecaps, no raging seas, no sinking sailboats, no indigo skies. Just serene seas and sailboats. And always beautiful. She thought Hannah was well on her way to her dream of becoming a professional artist.

"They took her away," Tim said, softly.

A sting, a jab to her heart. "Who took her away?"

"Her mom and dad." He blobbed dark spots on his white cow. "She got all better."

And the words jolted Zoe and echoed deep inside her. She got all better? How? That's not possible. She was sick. She was dying.

Zoe knelt down beside Tim and placed her hands on his shoulders. "Tim, look at me."

He stopped painting and looked at her. His eyes. So innocent. So truthful.

"You mean her parents came and took her so she could finish her final days at home?" she asked. "Is that what you mean?"

"Yeah, they took her home," he said. "But they took her because she got better."

She slowly took her hands from his shoulders and sat down in the chair next to him. She held her head in her hands, and she thought she heard Tim ask her if she had a headache, but she was so deep in her thoughts that she wasn't sure if he had said anything at all, and even if he had, she really didn't care to answer anyway.

And the thoughts poured in. All the things she should have said to Hannah. Told her to keep the dream alive. That's she's going to make it someday. And what she would have said to Hannah's mom. Sorry, she would say, for being so impatient with you in the shop. Had she known, she would have done things differently. And she wondered why she hadn't anyway.

Then she thought about the wish she had granted for Hannah when she saw her rubbing her guardian angel necklace.

Wishes.

Maybe they really do come true.

***

Zoe knew she was in a twenty-five-mile-per-hour zone, but she pushed the pedal down to thirty-five. She had to speed. This was survival. She reached for her cell phone and spoke Gabriel's name.

"You're not going to believe this," she said once he'd answered.

"Well, from the tone in your voice," he said, "I'd say Vanessa's following you again."

"Along with her entourage. Should we meet at the library again?"

"No."

"Then where?"

A pause.

"Gabriel?"

"Let her come."

"What? Are you crazy?"

"Probably." He paused, and in that pause, she thought he was about to change his mind, but then he said, "I'll see you and Vanessa and her gang in a few."

Zoe tossed her cell phone into her tote and thought back to that phone conversation she had with him after their first meeting. The words he'd spoken, "Don't tell anyone about the meetings," had sent chills up her spine.

So, Gabriel, what the hell are we doing?

Zoe drove into the lot and parked close to the front door, and like the library encounter, Vanessa seemed to hesitate before turning into a space just inside the entrance.

Zoe ran inside and immediately spotted Gabriel. She was about to approach him, but something held her back. The kids. How odd they seemed tonight. How enchanted they seemed with Gabriel. They stood around him as though he was about to give them each a gift of great value. Emily clapped, and Michael grinned a devilish grin. She caught Jamie's eye, and Jamie winked at her, a wink that said, *Nobody messes with any one of us, especially with the new kid.*

Zoe forced a smile, not so sure if she wanted to stay or run. The energy in the room shifted, like small electrical circuits zigzagging throughout, zapping her every now and then as though telling her that something quite extraordinary was about to unfold. And to please stay.

She felt anticipatory, and a cautious curiosity created a strong hold on her. Whenever she had had these feelings before, she had run. But this time, she listened, and this time she was not going to allow fear to rule. She felt the warrior within rise. And only a tiny bit of doubt.

"You all understand?" Gabriel asked the kids.

"We do!" they chimed.

He hustled over to Zoe and put his hands on her shoulders. "Relax. We're going to have showtime."

"Showtime?"

He smiled, and she thought he looked wicked. Deliciously wicked.

He turned to the kids and reached out his hands like a ringmaster about to start the circus. "Positions, please," he said.

"Wait a minute," she said, grabbing his arm. "What about Joanna?"

"I'm in charge of group tonight. Don't worry. Have some fun with this for a change. It can be fun, you know."

A sudden stillness engulfed the room as the kids moved into their positions. It was as though she was about to see the opening night to a spectacular Broadway show. She scanned the room, watching the kids, her friends, as they took their positions, like actors on a stage, and slowly, the show began to unfold.

Michael stood in the middle of the room, straight and proud. He held out his hands and lifted them up ever so slightly. Then, his hands looked as though he was pouring liquid gold from one hand into the other. A beautiful stream of gold. Jamie's hands glowed, too, rays of yellows, and Melissa's hands glowed pink. Emily's hands glowed emerald and purple, and the colors weaved through and around her, and she twirled and twirled around in the colors.

Beautiful. A bit unnerving, but beautiful.

Gabriel stood by the window.

Waiting.

Zoe wished that she could do what the other kids were doing. She'd love to freak out Vanessa too. But she didn't have what they had, so she just waited alongside Gabriel. But then she thought about what Tim had said about her hands. She held them up, looked at them, and concentrated.

Nothing.

Harder.

Nothing.

Okay, that was stupid, she thought, dropping her hands. *Tim was definitely hallucinating.*

And then the words of her math teacher, Mrs. Fleming, echoed to her: "It will fall into place . . . persistence . . . self-fulfilling prophecy . . . that's when the real magic happens . . . "

Zoe held her hands up again. She looked at them, only this time she just looked, without strain, without concentrating, without any pressure to see or feel any result. She simply relaxed and breathed. And waited. And breathed. And waited. *Patience.* That was another word Mrs. Fleming had used.

Then, she thought she saw something. Something ever so subtle. She looked at the palms of her hands. A glow, and slowly it grew brighter, then spread over her palms, up her fingers to her fingertips, then around her hands. A beautiful, soft golden glow. Then, purple dots danced in, through and around the glow, and her hands glowed as though breathing, an ebb and flow of energy.

My god, my hands look and feel beautiful. Absolutely beautiful.

She felt breathless. And now, she knew. She knew she was the one.

She looked at Gabriel with a huge smile, and slightly waved her hands, afraid that if she waved too fast, the glow would disappear, but his gaze was steadfast on the doorway. What was he staring at? She looked over her shoulder.

There stood Vanessa, her eyes wide and staring, her face drained of color. Her hands, how they trembled. She just stood there. Not a move. Not a flinch. Except for those hands. Zoe had never seen the invincible Vanessa Wellington look so fearful, and for a moment, she actually felt sorry for her.

Zoe watched as Vanessa backed away from the entrance, and no sooner had she disappeared around the corner than the kids heard a high-pitched, earsplitting scream.

The kids stopped their shenanigans. Zoe wondered if perhaps they hadn't overdone it, but by the enthusiasm of the kids racing to the window and pushing and shoving each other to get a good view, she didn't think so. She ran to the window, too, and stood on tiptoe behind the others.

"What's she doing?" Michael asked Gabriel.

"She's running really fast and her arms are in the air and she's flailing them all around." Gabriel paused. "She's standing by her car now and jumping up and down, her hands are moving all over the place, and her mouth is moving even faster. She's getting into her car, she's still talking. Wait. Meagan is getting out of the backseat. She's pulling Vanessa out of the driver's seat and Vanessa is trying to push her away, but Meagan is grabbing her by the arms and shoving her into the back. Meagan is shutting the back door and climbing into the driver's seat. She's driving off."

The kids jumped up and down and clapped their hands. "We did it. We did it. We did it!"

They laughed and hooted and hollered. They jostled and hugged one another, and they laughed and laughed and laughed some more, just like little kids. Happy little kids. Even Gabriel. A happy little-big kid.

For the first time, Zoe felt a strong bond with the kids, and she had comfort in knowing that she was like them after all. Everything was falling into place, and everything was feeling okay now. But how long would this feeling last?

***

Zoe grabbed a slice of pizza and a soda and joined Hailey and Isabelle at their table. Isabelle prattled on about getting first chair and about how she was preparing for a solo for the school concert next month. Hailey tried to one-up Isabelle's talent in music with her talent in sports.

"It's so intense!" Hailey said. "You wouldn't believe what they're having us do."

"Anyone can run, Hailey," Isabelle said.

"It takes tremendous strength and endurance to do what I do," Hailey said.

"Seriously, where's the talent in running?" Isabelle asked.

"Really?" Hailey said. "And how much talent does it take to blow?"

"Would you two stop it," Zoe said. "You're giving me a headache."

Zoe wondered how she could have two such different friends. Sometimes they irritated her with all their bragging about music and sports. She thought about her own talents, and how she'd finally decided on two pieces for the upcoming art show. She would enter a landscape of the Colorado mountains and aspens, and the other, her warrior princess. She was about to pull her warrior from her portfolio to show them her work when she got a whiff of Vanessa's perfume.

Zoe watched as Vanessa, Meagan, Tiffany, and Claire walked past their table and took their seats at the center table, just as they did every lunch hour. But this time, something was different. Today, Meagan led the gang to the table and sat where Vanessa usually sat.

"Hey, what's up with that?" Zoe asked, tilting her head toward the gang.

"I heard they took a vote," Isabelle said.

"A vote?" Zoe said.

"Didn't you hear?" Hailey said. "Vanessa got all freaked out about something last night and they voted to remove her as the head of the gang, so now Meagan is. She sits in Vanessa's spot now."

"Really?" Zoe said.

"I wonder what freaked her out so bad," Isabelle said.

"You know how they are," Hailey said. "The Gospel Girls. They're not about to tell anyone what happened."

"Thank god," Zoe said, realizing too late that she had spoken aloud.

"What?" Isabelle asked.

"Nothing."

The truth would have to wait, but for how long? How much longer could she keep up her ruse? She knew that eventually the truth reveals itself, whether you want it to or not, whether you're ready for it to or not. She could only hope that when the time came, she'd be ready.

Twenty-Five

As the school year progressed, Zoe's grades improved, which impressed her teachers and her mom, but caused discord between her and her friends. The invitations to parties became few and far between. Zoe knew they were still partying. Just not with her. And it wasn't that she so much cared about the partying, as much as it was the feeling of being snubbed by her friends. She wondered if perhaps the time had come for her to try again to tell them the truth.

And she decided that she would. Tomorrow. In school. Before first bell.

***

Zoe hustled down the sidewalk to the steps leading to the school entrance. She had awoken later than planned. By twenty minutes. Today of all days. She'd have to hurry if she wanted to talk with Hailey and Isabelle before the first bell sounded.

Halfway up the steps, she spotted Hailey and Isabelle

entering the school. She was about to call out to them, but was jolted by that saccharin voice with its coo-like lilt.

"Have you heard the news?"

Zoe watched as her friends disappeared, the double doors closing behind them. She let out a sigh of defeat before turning to face Vanessa and her entourage, and even though Meagan was still head of the Gospel Girl Gang, Vanessa had positioned herself slightly in front of her.

"What news?" Zoe asked, impatiently.

"My mom just called," Vanessa said, waving her cell phone, "about that internal investigation going on at the hospital."

"What about it?" Zoe asked.

"Your aunt's doctor friend is a fraud and she's been covering for him."

"That's a lie," Zoe said. She turned and started back up the steps.

"The news doesn't lie," said Meagan.

"Yeah, the news doesn't lie," said Tiffany.

Vanessa continued, "Your aunt is being hauled over to the administration building for questioning."

As much as Zoe wanted to ignore Vanessa's comment and keep climbing the steps, she stopped. Her brain went fuzzy. *Maggie's in trouble? How can that be? She didn't do anything wrong.* Maggie's words came back to her: "We have a situation here." And those two men, the stocky man and the dark-haired man. That's why they were at the hospital. Investigating that situation. An apparent cover-up situation.

She turned around and once again faced Vanessa. Oh,

how she felt like reaching out and shoving her, sending her tumbling down the steps. That would take that smug look off her face. And this time, Zoe would be able to reach. After all, she stood on the higher step and they were almost eye level now, and in that moment she noticed something about Vanessa she'd never noticed before. One of Vanessa's eyes was a bit higher than the other. A small defect in the ever-so-perfect Vanessa Wellington. Zoe smiled in satisfaction.

"Something funny, Web?" Vanessa asked.

Without answering, Zoe sprinted down the steps to her car, but not before yelling back, "Your offspring will look like trolls!"

She sped out of the parking lot, tires squealing, and headed toward the road to the hospital. Once outside the school zone, she pushed the pedal down and cursed at slow-moving cars and red lights. She pulled a Hailey by zipping through a yellow-turned-red, and before long, she was pulling into the hospital parking lot.

She drove past media vans.

Media? Seriously?

She screeched to a stop in a space reserved for handicapped parking. Right now, she didn't care. She needed convenience, not a conscience. Camera crews and newscasters swarmed the area along with police officers trying to control the crowd.

She spotted her aunt being led away from the hospital by the dark-haired man, his hand on her arm. The stocky man pushed the reporters aside. "Get that microphone out of my face!" he yelled.

Zoe pushed and shoved her way through the crowd. A guy and a gal swore at her, one woman said something about kids these days, a guy lost his balance and fell. She stepped on and over him while quickly apologizing, then raced up the steps.

"Wait, wait!" Zoe yelled. "Don't take her away! It was me! It was me!"

A man leaned out from behind his television camera. A reporter looked up from her notes and stopped talking long enough to turn to see what the cameraman was staring at. Everyone stopped. And stared. A sudden hush fell over the crowd. A stillness in the air. Even the breeze seemed to stop.

"Zoe, what are you doing here?" Maggie asked.

"Trying to save you."

"There's nothing you can do," Maggie said. "They've already made up their minds."

"You heard her, kid," Stocky said. "There's nothing you can do. Now run on like a good little girl and let us handle this."

Dark-Haired Man kept his grip on her aunt's arm. They descended the steps, and the reporters scrambled to get close to them.

"Yes," Zoe whispered. "There is something I can do."

She turned to face the crowd, the news crew, the police, and the hospital staff who had gathered to witness the hauling away of one of their own. She tilted her head back and closed her eyes. She took a deep breath and brought her hands to her chest, where she held them while continuing to breathe deeply. She took another breath and extended her hands and held them up. And held them and held them.

And wondered. She felt her hands grow warm and tingly, then an intense heat penetrated her palms, extending into her fingers, a fine point between pain and pleasure, more intense now, and she wanted to scream, the pain and pleasure was so intense, but she stifled her scream and continued to hold up her hands.

A woman screamed as though screaming for her.

Zoe slowly opened her eyes.

The woman pointed at her.

Maggie turned and Zoe met her gaze. A gaze of wonder and horror. A gaze that softened into a knowing.

Zoe looked at her hands. They glowed golden. Purple dots slowly appeared and swirled around and through the golden glow. But this glow was different than when she had scared Vanessa. This time the golden glow with the purple swirling dots stretched out far beyond her fingertips.

My god, how far can this energy go?

And in that moment, fear engulfed her and in that fear, the energy tightened and folded back toward her like a scroll rolling itself up. She relaxed, breathed, and relaxed some more and breathed some more and settled back into that blissful energy. Then, the golden hue and purple dots began to slowly emerge again from her fingertips, slowly stretching out before her.

I can actually control this.

She looked out over the crowd. Everyone had stopped doing whatever it was they had been doing and were now staring at her, but then a voice yelling "Zoe, no!" shattered the quiet hush of the crowd.

It was too late. She couldn't stop now. She had to continue for Maggie's sake. She held up her glowing hands for the crowd to see. Some appeared frightened and stepped back, and some moved in close, some closer, and some even closer. She felt hands on her body, hands touching her shoulders, her cheek—she instinctively brushed the hands away. One man knelt down and touched her feet. She screamed and stepped back as though burned by hot coals. Her legs shook and her whole body felt like it was melting. A tingly sensation swept through her, and she felt herself falling, falling, falling. Strong arms grabbed her and wrapped around her, shielding and protecting her. She looked up. Gabriel. That expression. She'd never seen that look in his eyes before.

"You've revealed us, Zoe," he whispered, holding her tight.

And before she could ask, shadows grew long and darkness enveloped her.

***

Zoe rested comfortably in her hospital bed, surrounded by her family. And Gabriel.

Diagnosis: stress.

The cure: rest.

Gabriel sat on the edge of the bed, resting his hand on hers. Together they watched the television news story unfold of Ms. Zoe Weber and her miraculous healing abilities. Christopher, dressed in his Superman shirt and red cape, sat on Nicole's lap twirling her blond hair through his fingers, oblivious to what was happening.

"Yeah, healing would be miraculous," Zoe said.

Gabriel grinned and gave her hand a gentle squeeze.

Zoe's mom flipped through the channels. "My god, Zoe," she said, "you're on every news station." She stopped flipping and settled on one.

"It seems rather coincidental," the news anchor said, "that patients improved so drastically after their attending physician, Dr. Scott Swanson, was transferred to another department."

"It did seem strange to us too," Stocky said, "which is why we had to do an internal investigation to be sure that Dr. Scott Swanson was indeed performing his job with the utmost of integrity, and that Dr. Margaret Ellis wasn't covering up for someone's incompetence."

The anchorman continued, "And so now we know what?"

Dark-Haired Man said, "We believe that both Dr. Scott Swanson and Dr. Margaret Ellis did conduct themselves ethically and professionally, and that the drastic improvement in the health of the patients may possibly have to do with a Ms. Zoe Weber." He paused. "It appears as though she's a healer, a modern-day miracle worker."

The anchor turned to Stocky. "And so none of this had anything to do with one doctor being negligent and another doctor covering that up?" he asked.

"Absolutely not," Stocky said.

Dark-Haired Man looked at Stocky, then at the anchor. "We don't believe so," he said.

And on and on they talked. Zoe grew tired with all the talk.

"Isn't that anchorman Robert McCarthy?" Charles asked. "Meagan's dad?"

Zoe shifted and leaned toward the TV. "Yeah, it is."

"What ever happened to Meagan?" Mom asked. "You two used to be such good friends."

Zoe leaned back. "She got some kind of cool."

"Now you've got some kind of cool," Nicole said, smiling proudly at her sister.

But Zoe wasn't so sure this was the kind of cool she wanted. To be the one. The healing one. The thought of that kind of power made her feel uncomfortable and anxious. She didn't know what to think, but what she did know was that she needed to have a talk with Gabriel. Alone.

"Charles," she said, "will you drive my car home, providing it hasn't been towed by now? Gabriel can give me a ride."

Christopher gave Zoe a kiss good-bye, his long, dark lashes tickling her cheek. "You going to get all better?" he asked.

"Yes, Christopher," Zoe said. She couldn't help but smile at his Superman shirt and red cape. "I am going to get all better."

"No cane this time?"

She smiled and shook her head.

"Come on, Christopher," Mom said. "Zoe has to rest."

"Mrs. Weber?" Gabriel said, getting up. "I know this must be very confusing for you and your family."

"To say the least." She looked at her daughter. "We'll talk more when you get home," she said, with a reassuring smile.

She then extended her hand to Gabriel in a warm handshake. "Thank you, Gabriel, for helping Zoe, even though I'm not sure what it is that you've done to help her." She shook her head. "This really is quite confusing."

"Mom," Zoe said. "It'll be okay. *I'll* be okay."

Charles wrapped his arm around his wife's shoulder and gently guided her out of the room. Nicole took Christopher's hand in hers and followed.

Zoe sat silently, rubbing her hospital bracelet. She didn't know how to start. She felt relieved when Gabriel started for her.

"How do you feel about all this?" he asked.

"You sound like a therapist."

"Sorry, I didn't mean to."

She let out a heavy sigh and stared at the ceiling tiles, wishing for paintings of butterflies there. "I don't know if I can handle this. It is me. It's me." She laughed a you-got-to-be-kidding-me laugh. "I can deal with the math thing, but I'm not so sure I can deal with this healing thing."

He wrapped his hands around hers. "You'll be okay, Zoe. Everyone's experience with an NDE is different, complicated."

"You can say that again," Zoe said. "Gabriel, why did you say something about revealing us?"

He took a deep breath. "Some people feel threatened by what we do," he said, "and because they feel threatened, they sometimes wish to harm us."

Threatened? Harm? People actually don't want us to heal others? How insane is that?

One question turning into hundreds.

This was getting exhausting.

"So, what about Dylan?" she asked. "He showed up at the group. And Vanessa."

"Some, I will admit, we scare for the fun of it," he said. "I don't think of Dylan or Vanessa as being threats."

"And that's what you meant by, 'You've revealed us?' because that scared me, Gabriel. In revealing the truth and saving Maggie, did I do something I shouldn't have?"

"You revealed us. I didn't say you betrayed us."

"Revealed. Betrayed. It sounds the same to me."

"You did what you had to do, but I want you to understand that there can be consequences."

Consequences in revealing the truth? She only knew of consequences in a lie. And now, she felt more confused than ever, because for once in her life she felt like she had done the right thing. She decided right then, once she was out of the hospital, that would be it. No more. No more hospitals. No more patients. She wasn't into this medical thing, anyway. That was her aunt's thing and her sister's thing. And her grandma's thing. Not hers. And it never ever would be, could be. Even with the art program. Besides, she'd finished her community service. She was off the hook, no longer responsible for any more patients or artists.

A thousand questions raced through Zoe's mind as Gabriel drove her home, but she decided she would ask him all those questions later. She leaned her head back and listened to the relaxing sounds of the classical station. She never would've figured him for a classical listening kind of guy, but then she figured that there were probably a lot of things she didn't know about him.

He turned down her street, but at the third block, he quickly braked.

She looked out the window, then at him. "This isn't my house. It's at the end of the street."

"You have company," he said, pointing down the street.

Media vans had parked in front of her house, and reporters and camera crews stood on the lawn.

"Keep driving," she said. "Turn down the side street, and I'll sneak in through the back." She laughed. "Just like I used to."

He smiled. "I'm glad you have a sense of humor about all this."

She ducked down and he continued driving.

"I could stop," he said. "Right here in front. You could get out and say hello."

"Gabriel! My humor isn't that intact. Keep driving."

"Sorry," he said, chuckling.

He turned the corner, then parked. "You can come up now," he said.

She sat up and pushed her hair away from her eyes. "Why can't they leave me alone?"

"You're a hot commodity now, Zoe. Come on. I'll walk you to the door."

"Want to stay for dinner?" she asked as they got out of the car.

"That'd be great. I'm starving."

They climbed over the chain-link fence and cut across

the yard. She pushed the sliding glass door open, and as they stepped into the dining room, she heard Charles at the front door with a tone in his voice she'd never heard before.

"She's been through enough," Charles said. "Now, if you'll please respect our privacy and leave. No, she doesn't want to make a statement." Pause. "I just did."

He closed the door with a bit more force than Zoe was used to hearing him do. She rushed to him, stood on her tiptoes, and gave him a quick peck on the cheek.

"Thanks," she said.

"They're relentless," he said, wrapping his arms around her. "Hopefully, they won't be back." He stroked her hair. "How are you feeling?"

"Hungry," she said, with a bright smile.

"Good," he said, smiling back. "Dinner will be ready shortly."

She looked at him and wondered if he felt as exhausted as he looked. His hair was disheveled and his smile seemed forced. Had the reporters been harassing him?

She suddenly felt sad. Scared. She had revealed herself, and in that revelation she hadn't thought about how this would affect her family. She was beginning to have second thoughts about what she had done. She had done the right thing, hadn't she?

Charles breezed past her and extended his hand to Gabriel. "Thanks for bringing her home," he said, giving him one quick handshake and a few pats on the shoulder. "You're welcome to stay for dinner."

Zoe brushed the thoughts away and smiled at Gabriel,

then Charles. "Well, that's good, because I've already invited him."

Later, at the table, Zoe dished up her third helping of zucchini lasagna, one of her favorite home-cooked meals, but only after she had already eaten a seaweed salad, three pieces of garlic bread, and tapioca pudding for old times' sake.

"Whoa, slow down, Zoe," her mom said with a chuckle. "I don't remember the last time you ate so much."

"I like to see a girl eat," Gabriel said, passing the garlic bread to Charles. "A healthy appetite is A-OK with me."

"Me too!" Christopher said, waving his forked zucchini in the air.

"Gabriel, we're so glad you were able to join us for dinner," Mom said, putting her hand on Christopher's, slowly lowering his hand to the table.

"Thank you for having me," he said.

Christopher pulled the zucchini from his fork and popped it into his mouth. "You welcome."

Zoe took a breath, and in that breath she realized how lucky she was to be surrounded by such a loving family, and her friend, Gabriel. She wondered where she would be without them. How would she have survived the past few months?

For the first time in a long time, she felt a sense of all things familiar sweep through her, weaving and binding her close to her family once again.

"Zoe," her mom said, "there's something you need to know."

She looked at her mom.

"You aren't the only one in the family who has the gift of healing," she said.

"Grandma?" Zoe asked.

Her mom nodded.

Nicole wiped sauce from her mouth. "Seriously, Mom. Grandma was a healer too?"

"She was, and a truly incredible one," Mom said. "But it wasn't easy for me and your aunt Maggie. The teasing from the kids at school, the church not wanting anything to do with us, the community eyeing us with suspicion . . . and all your grandmother wanted to do was to help people."

Gabriel looked at Zoe, then her mother. "If you don't mind my asking, Mrs. Weber, what exactly did your mother do?"

She sat silently for a moment, as though what she was about to say would send orderlies rushing in with straitjackets. When she finally found her voice, she said, "She was able to see the health issues in her clients by sensing their energy field. She used her hands to alter their energy, and by doing so, she was able to shift the energy and assist in their healing."

"She sounds like an incredible woman," Gabriel said.

"That's amazing," Nicole said.

"And that's why people came from all over to see her," Zoe said.

Mom nodded. "But I have to admit, the thought of another healer in the family scared me."

Zoe looked at her. "You knew?"

"When Maggie told me that her patients were leaving the hospital under very unusual circumstances, it was then that I thought it quite possible. We didn't want to say anything, not to you, not to anyone." She looked up at Charles, apologetically. "We wanted to be sure first."

He smiled at his wife, then at Zoe. "Having a healer in the family, to use Gabriel's phrase, is A-OK with me," he said, patting Zoe's hand.

Zoe looked at her stepdad. The peaceful and loving look in his eyes was back again.

"I believed you," Christopher said. "I did. I said I did. I always believed you."

Zoe smiled at Christopher. She wasn't so sure he understood what it was he actually believed, but right now she didn't care. A sense of serenity filled her, the warrior within now at peace, perhaps.

She caught Gabriel's eye and knew exactly what he was thinking. He nodded.

"Mom, Charles," she said. "Those meetings on Wednesdays. They're not what you think."

And just when she was about to tell them, the phone rang.

"Please not another reporter," Mom said, shaking her head in disgust. "How many is that?"

"I've lost count," Charles said, taking a sip of his wine.

"I'll get it," Nicole said.

"Thanks, Nicole," Mom said.

"Now, Zoe," said Charles. "What is it about your meetings?"

Zoe took a breath and began. She told Charles and her mom how she had met Gabriel, how he wasn't her tutor, how she was doing the math thing on her own, well, sort of on her own, and she explained the real purpose of the meetings. She told them how Aunt Maggie had suggested it and please don't be angry with her. She went on to tell them about the other kids who had NDEs and gifts and how awesome they all were, and just when she was about to apologize for all the lies, her mom interrupted.

"I'm sure all those kids are wonderful," she said, smiling at Zoe and Gabriel.

And in that moment of truth and understanding and believing, Zoe felt as though the warrior within was now dancing and rejoicing.

Nicole walked back into the dining room. "That wasn't another reporter," she said. "It was dad's girlfriend, Laurel. She'd like for me and Zoe to visit her and dad this weekend. Apparently, he's not doing so great."

But I've just been released from the hospital, Zoe thought. *I need my rest. I need time to exhale.*

And just like that, the warrior stopped dancing.

"We'll start packing tonight," Nicole said, sitting down.

"We?" Zoe said, dropping her fork on her plate with a ting. "What's with this 'we' crap? I'm not going. I'm not!"

She threw down her napkin and ran upstairs. She slammed her bedroom door, plopped down on her bed, and buried her face in her pillow. Soon after, someone softly knocked. The door squeaked open.

"Zoe," Gabriel said, "can I come in?"

She muffled out a "yeah" from deep within her pillow.

Gabriel sat down on the edge of her bed. "I'm not usually one to tell someone what to do," he said, "but it might be a good idea to visit your dad. It might be what he needs."

She turned over and leaned up on her elbow. "And what about what I need?"

"Zoe, maybe he wants to make amends."

"How noble of him. Making amends while on his deathbed."

"I don't think anyone said anything about him being on his deathbed."

She rolled back over on her stomach. "I know it would make him happy for me and Nicole to visit him"

"That's why you don't want to go? Because you know it just might make him happy and he never did anything to make you happy?"

She nodded and wiped away a tear.

"So at his most vulnerable time you want to hold out? Zoe, this isn't about winning or losing, or who's right and who's wrong." He paused. "Think about what Joanna said about understanding others."

She rolled over and sat up. "How can I possibly understand how a dad can be so abusive toward his family? How can I possibly understand how a dad could choose drugs and drinking and friends over his own family? How can I possibly understand that?"

How could he make her understand? What could he say? What could anyone say to ease the pain?

"I don't get it," she said. "Why do the ones who are

supposed to love you the most end up hurting you the most?"

"I can't answer that one for you."

"I'm not really asking you to." She paused. "Sometimes I feel like curling up and hiding for the rest of my life."

"Sometimes that does sound like a damn good idea." He brushed a strand of hair from her face. "With all the media madness, it might actually be good for you to get away for a while."

Silence.

He gave her socked foot a tender squeeze, then left as softly as he had entered.

She drifted off to sleep. An arched door stood in front of her. She walked up to the door and put her hand on the doorknob. It wouldn't turn. She put her palms against the door and pushed. It wouldn't budge. She leaned her body against the door and shoved. She shoved and shoved. It wouldn't move. She stopped. She relaxed. No more forcing. No more resisting.

And in that moment, the door slowly opened and a breeze blew in, bringing in the sweet scent of lavender, and she breathed in the sweetness. In that breath she felt relaxed, refreshed, rejuvenated. The breeze whispered to her, "Welcome back."

Zoe awoke with a start. *What was that all about?* she wondered. *Welcome back? Welcome back to what? Is anything ever going to make sense to me?*

So many thoughts came rushing in. Thoughts of her dad, the media, the hospital, all those patients,

patients-turned-artist, some leaving, some staying, her sanity, her friends, the new ones, the old ones. She wanted to scream, but instead took a deep, cleansing breath. She relaxed back into the softness of her pillow and gazed up at the ceiling. Above her hung one of her favorite figurines, a gothic fairy cloaked in purple with butterfly wings, and in her hand she held a white wand. Make a wish, it seemed to say.

"I wish," Zoe said, "that life didn't have to be so damn hard to figure out."

Twenty-Six

The following morning, Zoe pulled the curtain away from her bedroom window. No one from the media had camped out in their front yard. They were all gone. It was quiet once again. She ran downstairs and into the kitchen.

"Mom, do I have to go to school today?"

"I can certainly understand why you wouldn't want to," her mom said, pouring herself a cup of coffee. "It probably won't be easy for you now that the kids at school probably know."

"I don't care if they tease me," Zoe said. "I just need some time to process what's happening to me."

"I'll call the school."

Zoe grabbed a box of cereal from the cupboard. "I decided to go to Durango, so you might as well tell them I'll be out until Monday," Zoe said.

"That's a sudden change of heart," Mom said. "Gabriel?"

Zoe nodded.

"He's a good kid," Mom said, grabbing her purse and

car keys. "I need to get to the shop. Call me if you need anything."

"Thanks, Mom."

After her mom had left, Zoe called Dylan.

"I heard the news," he said. "Is it true?

"Can we get together?" she asked.

"Yeah, sure."

The October air was warmer than usual and the sun shone brightly. Zoe met Dylan at a park not far from her house. Together, they walked to a creek and sat on a large, flat boulder, warmed from the sun. The rays of the sun danced across the sparkling water. Mallards dipped below the surface for food. One mallard pecked at another. The duck pecked back, then swam away, spreading its wings and ruffling its feathers. The duck swam calmly now. All was well in his world again.

"So, you're a healer now," Dylan said.

"Something like that," she said. "I'm not so sure I want to be, though. I liked my life the way it was before all this. I'm not so sure about anything now."

"Not even us?"

"This doesn't change anything between us, Dylan."

He pulled out a pipe, lit it, and handed it to her.

"Dylan, I'm not doing that anymore."

He looked at her with a "you got to be kidding me" look. He took a hit, then put it back into his coat pocket. "Anything else I should know?"

She knew that life had given her a different road map now, and why did she feel as though she really didn't need to explain or justify or defend her new life to him?

"Nicole and I are going to Durango this weekend." She paused. "Come with us."

He sat silent for a while before answering. "I can't."

"Can't, or don't want to?"

"Can't, but I would like to see those stars you talked about," he said.

Zoe's head was spinning.

Where did she stand with him?

She leaned over and kissed him.

He kissed her back.

Only this time, the sparks didn't fly.

***

Nicole lugged her suitcase down the stairs with a *thumpity-thump*. Zoe followed, carrying a small duffel bag and tote. They tossed their luggage into the trunk of Nicole's Mustang, and hugged their mom, Charles, and Christopher good-bye. Christopher begged to go along. Zoe assured him that they were leaving for only a few days. He asked her if she would bring him back a present. After she assured him of that, too, they climbed into the Mustang. Zoe waved and waved to Christopher until he disappeared into the dip of the hill.

Nicole wanted to take Highway 285 for the scenic views, but Zoe wanted to hurry and thought I-25 would be faster, so after a quick round of rock-paper-scissors, Zoe let out a whoop, and Nicole headed for I-25.

"I need to know," Nicole asked. "Are you and Gabriel together?"

"We're friends." She looked at her sister and saw doubt. "It's the truth. About the only truth I've told lately." She took a long sip of her soda. "Besides, Dylan and I are back together again."

"Seriously?" Nicole said. "I can't believe you're still seeing him."

A long silence filled the air. Zoe wondered if her sister would ever understand her.

Nicole finally broke the silence. "I'm sorry I didn't believe you when you first tried to tell all of us about your near-death experience."

"I don't blame you or anyone else," Zoe said. "I mean, the whole NDE thing, having a gift like Grandma's, it's all kind of scary."

"I think it's kind of cool."

"I'm not so sure, but I do wish that I would have had a chance to tell Hailey and Isabelle." She turned and gazed out the window.

Nicole turned down the volume on the radio. "Why didn't you tell them?"

"Everything happened so fast. It doesn't matter. They don't call anymore, anyway."

"Kids can be so mean," Nicole said.

Zoe looked at her sister. "How would you know? You were one of the popular ones. Everyone liked you." She turned back to the dry landscape rushing past. "You have no idea how mean and how cliquey they are. You were too far into it."

A heavy silence fell, that awkward silence that only

existed when she rode along with her parents to and from court, or to and from a parent-teacher conference. Maybe her comment wasn't fair, but it was honest.

Nicole turned the volume back up on the radio. Zoe realized this conversation was over. She leaned back and thought about the transience of life, and before long, the rhythmic sound of the music slowly faded and so, too, did she.

Zoe awoke to see the San Juan Mountains looming in the distance. She stretched and yawned. "How far are we?"

"We just went through Alamosa, so about three more hours."

Zoe grabbed a bottle of water from the backseat, opened it, and took a swig. "I feel nervous about seeing Dad."

"Is it nerves, or is it guilt?"

"Guilt? Why would you think that I'd feel guilty?"

"Because maybe you don't really want to see him."

"I don't, but I don't feel guilty about that."

"I was just asking."

"Don't analyze me, Nicole." She pounded her fist on her seat. "Why do I feel like I need to find a mountaintop so I can scream?"

"You don't think having what Grandma had is something incredibly awesome and wonderful. There you go again, Zoe, being stubborn and unappreciative."

"I feel like I don't even know who I am anymore."

"Zoe, you know what your problem is?"

"Enlighten me, Miss Perfect."

"What?"

Zoe snapped off the radio. "You know what your problem is?" she asked, getting in her sister's face. "You think you're so damn perfect. You think you just know it all." She leaned back. "Pull over. I think I'm going to be sick."

Nicole quickly decelerated, and Zoe abruptly shifted forward and put her hand on the dash to steady herself. She felt the dip of the car as it moved from smooth pavement to bumpy shoulder. Nicole slammed on the brakes, kicking up a cloud of red dust. Zoe got out, coughed, and waved the red dust cloud away from her face.

"What the hell?" Nicole asked, getting out of the car and coming around to Zoe's side. "Where'd that come from? Look, we're just having a discussion here. No need to get so damn defensive."

"You call this a discussion?" Zoe asked, slamming her door shut. "I call it 'let's have Zoe fix Dad so all will be well with the world' bullshit!"

"At least I'd consider . . . no, I *would* use a gift like yours for Dad, regardless of the shit he pulled!"

"That's the difference between you and me. You're the one who has to always come to the rescue, the one who has to save everyone whether they want to be saved or not, whether they should be saved or not!"

Nicole got into Zoe's face now, finger pointing into her chest. "You're just like him, with your damn drinking and drugging and hanging out with the wrong crowd. You're headed down the same road he was and you know it and you can't stand the thought of it. Everything you hate about him, you are, were. Why the hell can't you see that?"

She pushed Nicole's hand away. "I'm not like him. I'm nothing like him. He was a lousy loser of a dad."

"No shit. That doesn't mean it's okay to be a lousy daughter."

"He's the adult. He should have acted like one."

"Zoe, I'm not excusing his behavior. I agree with you. But don't make excuses for your own behavior because of his."

Zoe kicked a rock and it skipped across the highway and disappeared over the edge of the road. She leaned against the car door. Maybe Nicole was right. She had been going down the same path as her father, but then something had happened, and she realized that that something wasn't an accident. She and almost everyone else had called it that to make sense of it. She wondered how the truth of an event, however unfavorable, couldn't be fully realized because we failed to fully understand it, and conveniently, called it something else. As much as Zoe wanted to believe otherwise, what had happened to her had needed to happen. Limp, scar, and all.

Fight intelligently, Charles always said. Don't take a bad situation and make it worse. Count to ten. She always thought that counting to ten was the dumbest thing ever. She had always counted to ten—well, usually only eight, and really, really fast—but always blew up anyway. This time she took a deep breath and counted slowly, all the way to ten.

"Nicole?"

"Yeah?"

"Do Dad and Laurel even know?"

"Only about the accident."

"Nothing else?"

"You know Mom and Charles. They don't tell Dad and Laurel much of anything, and besides, what makes you think they'd even believe any of this."

"I guess it does sound kind of crazy," Zoe said.

"They'd probably think we'd all gone crazy," Nicole said, "and never want to see us again."

"Maybe we should have told them," Zoe said.

Nicole chuckled. Zoe looked at her sister, who looked as though she was biting her cheek to keep from laughing. Zoe tried not to laugh, but a grunt came out and before she knew it, she was laughing right alongside her sister.

Then, Zoe grew quiet. She looked at the ground, shuffled her feet, kicked another rock, but not so hard this time. "I'm sorry," she said.

"Me too," Nicole said. "Now, come on." She tossed her car keys to Zoe. "You're driving."

"Seriously?"

"Just keep it to the speed limit."

And off they went. Zoe zipped down the highway. Nicole asked her to slow down, take it easy, and then she asked Zoe to tell her all over again about her visit with Grandma, and this time, she said, she would not only listen, but she promised to really hear her. So, Zoe told the story all over again, this time without interruption, this time being heard, this time being believed, and this time feeling okay—feeling very much okay.

***

Zoe maneuvered the Mustang down the bumpy dirt driveway. Mature oak trees lined the long driveway, and the leaves on the swaying branches shimmered white and gold in the light of the fading sun. She pulled alongside a rusted orange tractor that had probably seen the last of its field days. She looked toward the house. Chipped paint exposed the gray of the weathered two-story farmhouse with its Victorian-style porch. Baskets hanging from the porch had perhaps, in the warm months, held crimson geraniums.

The screen door squeaked open, and Laurel emerged in khakis and a white sweater. Her hair was much shorter than when they had seen her almost a year ago. Zoe thought her shorter, grayer hair with bangs set off her blue eyes. Sans makeup, she looked pretty. Laurel greeted them with a warm smile, but underneath that smile, Zoe detected strain and worry.

A chocolate Labrador followed closely on Laurel's heels.

"I'm so glad you were both able to come on such short notice," she said. "Do you need help with your bags?"

"We got it," Nicole said, reaching into the trunk and grabbing her suitcase. She handed Zoe her duffel bag.

"Are you hungry?" Laurel asked. "I can make sandwiches, and I have herbal tea."

The girls nodded.

"Come on inside. You too, Mocha," Laurel said.

White lace curtains fluttered in the breeze, casting purple shadows upon the buttery walls, and the late evening sun cast a golden hue across the rustic wood floors. A bouquet of sunflowers in a galvanized vase sat atop the mantle. The red-and-yellow plaid French country sofa and matching chair, leather recliner, and two wooden rocking chairs gave the room an inviting and relaxing, however cramped, feel. Zoe wondered why two people needed so much furniture. Beyond the living room was a den, to the left a hall leading to more rooms, and to the right, the kitchen.

"Nicholas, the girls are here," Laurel said, closing the living room window.

Their dad shuffled in from the kitchen, holding a steaming mug of coffee in one hand and a cane in the other. The blue robe he wore appeared to be a few sizes too big.

"Dad?" Nicole said.

Zoe and Nicole exchanged glances. The man who stood in front of them looked nothing like the man they had seen last Thanksgiving. His ashen face was sunken and wrinkled. The once towering frame, that in their youth had intimidated them, looked so small. But those eyes, those sapphire eyes that glistened with a teary wetness, were unmistakably their father's.

"Nicole, Zoe. It's so good to see you again," he said, handing his coffee mug to Laurel. "Come here and give your old man a hug."

Zoe looked at Nicole as if to say, *You first.*

Nicole walked over to her father and gave him a hug. She turned to Zoe as if to say, *Your turn.*

Zoe walked over and gave him a hug. *Bones. All I feel are bones. And he's shorter. So much shorter.*

Their father waved for them to have a seat on the sofa. "I'm so glad you were able to come," he said, sitting in the recliner. "How was the drive?"

Laurel handed Nicholas his mug, then disappeared into the kitchen.

Mocha plopped down by Zoe's feet. She leaned over and rubbed his ears.

Their father reached for a tissue and coughed a raspy, gurgled cough.

"Are you okay, Dad?" Nicole asked, leaning forward.

He coughed again. "I probably look and sound a lot worse than I really am. I'm actually doing a lot better than I was a week ago."

The girls looked at each other as if to say, *He was actually worse than this?*

Laurel returned with a tray of steaming tea, the scents of licorice, peppermint, and lemon filling the air. The girls each took a glass, thanking her.

"I'll leave the three of you alone to catch up on things," Laurel said. "If you need anything else, I'll be on the front porch."

Nicole squeezed her lemon slice into her tea, then dropped the lemon into her glass. She looked up at her father, hesitating. "Dad, what exactly is wrong with you?"

"Hard and stupid living is what's wrong with me," he said with a wave of his hand as though erasing the past. The light in his eyes seemed to diminish. He sat silently.

"Dad?" Nicole said.

He looked up as if someone had poked him. "Sorry. I get a little drifty sometimes."

That's nothing new, Zoe thought.

"What have you girls been up to?" he asked. "I want to hear all about it."

Zoe listened as Nicole talked about how she made the dean's list again, how she's changed her major again, how she's working at the country club again and saving for next semester, and on and on and on.

There she goes, monopolizing the conversation as usual.

"Nicole," their dad said, "would you hand me that blanket beside you?"

Nicole grabbed the blanket and gently placed it over her dad's lap, and as she straightened it out, she asked him if there was anything else she could get him, and in that moment, Zoe realized that that was her cue. She slipped out the front door. Mocha followed.

She found Laurel sitting on the front porch swing, one foot tucked under the other, reading a paperback.

"Mind if I join you?" Zoe asked.

Laurel looked up. "Everything okay in there?"

Zoe sat down. "Yeah."

"Well, that was convincing," Laurel said, tucking her bookmark into her paperback. "You can tell me."

She looked up at her. "Is Dad sick because of alcohol and drugs?"

"For the record, Zoe, your dad has been clean and sober for a little over a year now."

"That's a lie."

"Excuse me, young lady."

"I was here last Thanksgiving," Zoe said. "He was slurring his words and acting all stupid."

"Zoe, he wasn't being that way because of alcohol or drugs."

"You seriously expect me to believe that? He was drunk."

"You've probably rarely seen your dad sober, or not using, and I'm sorry for that. But I promise you, he was clean last time you saw him."

Zoe looked at her with piercing eyes. "That's a bunch of bullshit."

Zoe thought she saw hurt, surprise, shock in Laurel's eyes, but before Laurel could say anything, Zoe got up and ran down the porch steps to the cottonwood tree. She grabbed the tire swing.

This was her place. This tree. This swing. Whenever she visited her dad, she would spend hours on this swing, a peaceful retreat where she could think. What was this thing called childhood really? Sometimes it felt like nothing more than a cruel joke of the universe.

Perhaps there was no such thing as a happy childhood, and all those kids who said they had a happy childhood were perhaps the saddest kids of all, and the families who looked perfect were perhaps the most messed up of all. Dysfunction disguised as perfection.

But then Zoe remembered what Joanna had said: "The Universe is on your side, although it may not feel like it sometimes." A part of Zoe wanted to believe that, but it hadn't felt like it then, and it didn't feel like it now. What *did* make Zoe feel better was swinging, so she swung, and in her swinging her misery melted into the rays of the vanishing sun and her despair disappeared into the depths of the darkening sky.

She heard the softness of Laurel's voice. "Zoe, please, I'm telling you the truth."

Zoe slowed her swinging.

Laurel continued, "By the time he decided to quit the drugs and alcohol, it was too late. His liver and kidneys had been so compromised."

Zoe stopped swinging. She poked her toe into the dirt. A long silence passed before she finally asked, "Is he going to be okay?"

"We don't know," Laurel said.

Zoe twirled around and faced her. "Why are you with him, anyway?" Then, she twirled back around as though the answer didn't matter.

"I've known your dad since high school. I liked him very much, but the feeling was never reciprocated."

The words jolted Zoe. She turned back around. "You were in love with my dad way back then?"

Laurel sat down on the grass. "He chose your mom, and your mom is a wonderful woman, but codependent relationships don't help in the push and pull of trying to get out of the muck. She realized she had to leave him, and she did, for you and Nicole."

Mocha lazily plopped down next to Laurel. She scratched his ear.

"I love your father in a way that transcends a romantic love," Laurel said. "It's hard to explain. But I knew I wanted him back in my life, and I knew I wanted to take care of him."

"Change him, you mean?" Zoe asked.

"No, not change him. You can't change anyone," Laurel said. "Don't even try unless you actually enjoy feeling frustrated."

Zoe kicked at the dirt. "Why did any of this even have to happen?"

"The person who has gained wisdom is the person who stops asking why," Laurel said.

"Then I'm never going to gain wisdom," Zoe said. "I'm doomed."

Laurel laughed. "I hardly doubt you're doomed, Zoe."

A breeze caressed Zoe's face. "Laurel?"

"Yes."

"I never did thank you and Dad for the bouquet of stargazers and irises," Zoe said. "They were beautiful."

"You're welcome," Laurel said. "I wish your dad and I could have been there."

"I understand now why you weren't."

"I'm glad you're doing so much better since your accident." She stood and extended her hand to Zoe. "Let's go back in. It's getting cool. You too, Mocha."

Zoe took Laurel's hand, and they walked toward the house. Perhaps she was too old to be taking another's hand, but right now, she didn't care. Laurel's hand felt warm and safe in hers, and she decided that she really did like Laurel, even though she wanted to correct her about using the word *accident*.

Twenty-Seven

Zoe awoke to the sounds of jays squawking, chickens clucking, squirrels chattering, and Mocha barking. She wondered how anyone could sleep with all that noise. She rolled over and looked at Nicole's bed. Apparently, her sister had already figured that one out. She quickly threw on her sweats and ran downstairs and into the kitchen.

A potbelly stove sat in the corner, and Zoe wondered if Laurel actually cooked with that thing. A drying rack next to the sink held a few dishes and cups. Not even a dishwasher. Folk art of roosters covered the walls. Open shelves held the dinnerware, cookware, and canned and sacked food.

Laurel dished up scrambled eggs and blueberry pancakes. "Good morning, Zoe. Did you sleep well?"

Zoe sat down on the wooden bench across from Nicole. The table looked like a recycled door, and she wondered if there wasn't anything that Laurel and her dad didn't recycle and reuse.

She looked up at Laurel. "Yeah, I did. Thanks."

"Isn't Dad joining us for breakfast?" Nicole asked.

"He's resting," Laurel said. "After breakfast, I'll pack a lunch for the three of you." She put a bowl of blueberries on the table. "Your dad would like for you to take him to Vallecito Lake today."

"Where's that?" Nicole asked.

Laurel sat down in the captain's chair at the head of the table. "About twenty miles northeast in the San Juan National Forest," she said. She spooned fresh blueberries onto her pancakes.

"You're not going?" Zoe asked.

"I think it's important for the three of you to spend some time together without me," Laurel said.

"Nicole can take him," Zoe said, pouring syrup on her pancakes.

Nicole and Laurel looked at Zoe.

Zoe sensed their stares and looked up. "What?"

Laurel lowered her fork. Her bite of blueberries would have to wait. "Zoe, I think you should go."

"I'd rather stay here with you."

"Well, you can stay, but I'm hosting book club at noon. We'll be discussing *Olive Kitteridge* by Elizabeth Strout. You will join us."

Zoe looked at her sister. "What time did you want to leave?"

After breakfast, Laurel placed the picnic basket in the trunk of Nicole's car. She tenderly kissed Nicholas good-bye and helped him into the front seat. Zoe climbed into the back.

"Drive safely," Laurel said.

After directions from Dad, Nicole headed northeast out of Durango toward the lake.

"Vallecito Lake is in a secluded mountain valley," he said, "and is perhaps the most beautiful lake in all of Colorado." He told stories of when he and Laurel went hiking and mountain biking around the lake, and stories of renting horses and trail riding.

"Those days are long over now," he said.

"Are you able to get out much, Dad?" Nicole asked.

"Unfortunately, not as much as I'd like to, so this is a real treat." He glanced toward the backseat. "Hey, Zoe, you're awfully quiet. Everything okay?"

"I'm good," Zoe said. She knew it didn't sound convincing. She didn't care.

Nicole continued on County Road 501, and as soon as they rounded the bend, the full beauty of Vallecito Lake was displayed magnificently before them. Zoe leaned forward, resting her hand on the back of her father's seat, and gawked out the window. The crystal blue lake shimmered in the sunlight, and the verdant forest and the mountains and the hills seemed to break forth into song. Zoe thought the scenery even more beautiful than that of the mountain drives not far from home, and she was beginning to feel glad she had come, but she wasn't about to tell her dad that.

Once at the park, they settled at a table nestled among a cluster of ponderosa pines. Their dad popped open two sodas and handed them to his daughters. Zoe was about to take a sip, but a strong breeze blew through her hair, and the scent of lavender filled the air. She looked out across the valley. Lavender swayed in the breeze. She put her soda down and walked toward the edge of the steep hillside. The blues of the lavender field faded into the blues of a pond, which faded into the blue sky. One vast sweep of blue.

"Zoe, everything okay?" Nicole asked.

"I just want to check this out."

A stronger breeze blew. She took a deep breath, stretched out her arms, and reached toward the sky. She was about to call out to Nicole to come see this, smell this, feel this, but Nicole and Dad were talking and laughing. Then suddenly, she could no longer hear them.

That's weird, she thought. *I heard them only a moment ago talking about how Laurel forgot to pack the pickles.*

She turned and watched as Nicole placed napkins and plastic cups on the picnic table. Another strong breeze whipped around Zoe. The napkins remained still. The plastic cups remained still. Why was everything so still, so silent? Except for where she stood?

She turned back toward the valley. She felt an exhilarating warmth flow through her. She tilted her head back, reached out her arms, and embraced the energy, whatever this energy was, and felt an intense sense of peace and love.

She thought she heard a voice. A soft, sweet voice. A familiar voice.

Things to do, the voice whispered. *It all matters.*

The breeze diminished. She strained to hear that voice, that whispering voice, but it was gone. She dropped her arms. The breeze was gone. She stood, staring at the valley, the pond, the lavender.

"Did you hear me? Zoe?" Nicole called.

Zoe turned to look at her sister and her dad.

"Are you going to stand there all day?" Nicole asked, hands on hips. "I could use some help here."

Zoe hustled over to the picnic table. "You should have seen that. It was awesome," she said, blurting out the words faster than she wanted to, because the last thing she wanted was for her dad to know that she did like this place and that she was glad she had come.

Dad smiled. "This is one of my favorite places, and now you know why. I'm so grateful the two of you were able to bring me here. I'm glad you like it too. Now, come on. Let's eat."

Zoe unwrapped her turkey club guacamole sandwich, passed on Dad's homegrown tomatoes, but scooped up Laurel's homemade potato salad loaded with fresh dill, also from their garden.

Nicole looked up. Zoe caught her glance.

"What?" Zoe asked.

"You look pale," Nicole said. "Paler than Dad, and that's pale."

"I'm okay. I just . . . " She stared at her food. She lightly tapped her plastic fork on her plate.

"Maybe it's the altitude," Dad said. "We are at eight thousand feet."

"It's not the altitude," Zoe said.

"You're not okay, then?" Dad asked.

"I'm not feeling quite right."

"It's Dylan, isn't it?" Nicole said. "We've been here one day and already you're lovesick."

"It has nothing to do with Dylan," Zoe said.

Dad turned to Zoe. "Who's Dylan?"

"Her boyfriend," Nicole said. "And he's one sorry messed-up dude."

Zoe looked at Nicole, eyes narrowing, "He is not messed up."

"According to Mom he is," Nicole said. "What do you see in a high school dropout, anyway?"

Dad put down his fork. "Girls, enough." He turned to Zoe. "Who's this Dylan guy everyone seems so upset about?"

And before she could answer, Nicole said, "He's the guy that put her in the hospital. Didn't Mom and Charles tell you?"

There she goes again with her mouth.

Dad brushed his hair back. "They only said she was in a car accident and that everything was all right and don't worry about coming and that they'd keep me posted."

Great. Now they're talking like I'm not even here. I think I would like to disappear right about now. Oh wait. As far as they're concerned, I already have. I really hate these two sometimes.

"Dad," Nicole said, "he almost got her killed."

Almost? We've already had that discussion too.

"What?" Dad dropped his fork. "Nobody told me that! Why didn't anyone tell me?"

He looked at Zoe, expectantly.

Her eyes glazed over and she felt them begin to burn. "Oh, like you think I should have called and told you?" Zoe said. "I was out of it for weeks."

"Well, no, Zoe, I didn't mean . . . I meant—"

"Mom said you were too sick to come," Nicole said.

"Your mom made it sound like she had nothing more than a scratch." Dad shook his head in disbelief. "Sounds like something she'd do. Downplay it to intentionally keep me away." He turned to Zoe. "I would have made it. I could have—"

"Like all those other times you said you'd make it?" Zoe said.

"Zoe!" Nicole said.

"Your shit was always more important to you," Zoe said. "You're lucky we even came here, because you don't deserve to even see us. You were never around, and when you were, you weren't, and my friends always asked me what was wrong with you, and how could I tell them that I had a stoner, alcoholic, wife-beater for a dad? I hate you! I hate you both!"

She pushed herself away from the table and raced to the steep hillside, where she half-climbed, half-tumbled down to the lavender field below, and she ran and ran and ran through the field, and the lavender spikes brushed against her legs, sending an intoxicating scent into the air. She thought she heard Nicole call her name. She didn't care.

Her lungs felt like fire, yet the running felt invigorating. She ran down a steep hill, and when she reached the pond, she plopped down, breaths coming hard. She drew her knees to her chest and lowered her head. She wanted the tears to come, but they wouldn't. Was it possible to be so sad that no tears could fall?

It was true. She did miss Dylan. No one understood him. No one understood her. No one understood how perfect they were for one another. Why couldn't anyone?

He needs you, Zoe.

"What?" She raised her head.

He needs you, the voice said again.

"What the hell?" She stood up and looked across the pond. "Who's there?"

A breeze blew over the pond, and droplets of water fell on her face. She wiped the drops from her forehead and her cheeks. She looked at her fingers. Gold and purple glistened from them.

"What the . . . ?"

She felt the breeze again, stronger this time, and she heard the voice again: *Seek to understand him, and your true gift of healing will be revealed.*

"Grandma? Is that you? I understand Dylan perfectly."

A sudden gust of wind hit Zoe hard. She wobbled and, unable to regain her balance, fell flat on her back. The strong wind subsided and a calm, gentle breeze arched the lavender spikes over her body as though embracing her.

"If that's you, Grandma, I think I got your message."

She got up and raced toward the hill, and when she reached it, she leapt up with such an athletic poise that she actually startled herself. She grabbed onto roots, and whatever else the good earth provided for her, and she pulled and pulled and pulled, willing herself toward the top. It was as if the good earth had met her with benevolent accommodation and anticipated, even expected, her every move.

Almost there.

Pulling up with her hands and pushing down with her feet, she was about to pull herself over the last part of the hill and rest when she saw a hand in front of her. She looked up and into the smiling eyes of her dad. She felt the strong grasp of his hand in hers as he yanked her up the last few feet. She felt shock and surprise at his strength, and she couldn't understand how he could be so sick and so strong at the same time.

"You okay, kid?" her dad asked.

She felt the firm earth under her feet, and a sense of security and wellness poured through her. She looked up at her dad. Should she tell him what happened out there? But how could she? She wasn't too sure herself. She already had him convinced, probably, that she wasn't okay. She felt that breeze again, a soft breeze that felt like a hand brushing across her cheek, caressing her ever so gently.

She looked at her dad. "I'm okay."

"You say you're okay, but can I believe you?"

Zoe looked at the ground.

"Zoe?"

"Dad, things have been kind of messed up ever since the accident, I mean incident, whatever. I was trying to tell you about everything before Nicole opened her mouth."

She grew silent.

"I'm listening," he said.

"It's just that . . ."

"What is it?"

"Hey, Zoe," Nicole said, running up to them. "Are you okay? Sorry if I upset you."

"I'll tell you later," Zoe said to her dad before turning to

Nicole. "Yeah, I'm okay."

"We should start cleaning up." Nicole said. "There's a storm moving in."

They headed to the picnic table, but Zoe turned to take one last look at the valley. She felt cold raindrops plop on her face, and this time, she didn't wipe them off. The wind had intensified and the lavender swayed in the breeze as though waving good-bye to her. She held up her hand and waved back. She stood for a moment in reverence of Nature. She watched as the sun's golden rays streamed through the gathering gray clouds, casting a glistening light on the surface of the still pond. She gave thanks for all of it, for the seen and the unseen, and then she whispered a prayer of gratitude for her grandma.

Twenty-Eight

Zoe tossed and turned. She glanced at the clock. Midnight. As much as she tried to stop the thoughts racing through her mind, her grandma's words only grew stronger: *He needs you.* And the words her grandma spoke to her in her NDE: *You have things to do.* The only interruption from her thoughts was an occasional sharp creak and loud pop from the walls of the old farmhouse.

A strong breeze rattled the open window. She rolled out of bed, pushed the window down, and latched it. She looked out. A crescent moon. And the stars. How brightly they shone through a black velvet canopy. She was wide awake now and decided that the stars were meant to be seen, but not through a window. She made her way downstairs, each step creaking as she went.

She passed the den, but the soft snores of her father gave her pause. She peered in. Mocha lay by his side, and upon seeing her, let out a lazy groan.

"Shhh, Mocha."

He let out a stifled bark.

"Go back to sleep," she whispered.

He plopped his head back down between his paws, then closed his eyes. She breathed a sigh of relief.

She looked at her father, sleeping so peacefully, and wondered where his dreams took him. Mountain biking? Hiking? Horseback riding?

She was about to head outside, but a strong scent filled the room.

Lavender? Okay, Grandma. You win.

She grabbed the three-legged wooden stool by the grandfather clock, placed it next to her father's bed, and sat. She rested her hand on her father's hand and waited. She heard the gust of the wind, an occasional creak in the walls, the ticking of the clock. And her heartbeat.

She waited. And waited. A heavy sigh. She scratched an itch at the back of her neck. She looked up at the clock. 12:40.

Perhaps this wasn't meant to happen.

She would wait a few more minutes, but that was it. She inhaled deeply, and in that breath, the musty sweetness of English lavender misted into the air. A gentle touch, now on her shoulder, a touch that moved down her arm, to her hand, and to her fingertips. And then, the sensation left her.

She looked at her father's hand again. Nothing. The ticking of the grandfather clock seemed louder, the popping and creaking of the house seemed louder, the gusting of the wind seemed stronger. She was about to leave, but then saw something. A golden glow slowly moved around her hand, then to her father's hand, up his arm, to his throat, then to his chest.

Mocha groaned, raised his head, and looked at her. He let out a wimpy bark.

"Go back to sleep, Mocha," she said, gently pushing his head down.

Mocha lowered his head, but looked up at her again.

"Okay, Mocha, if you must."

Zoe watched the golden light slowly undulate around her father's heart. The light appeared to be breathing in and out in the same rhythm as his breath. It hovered there for a while before moving back to his throat, then to top of his head. The light glowed there before moving toward the ceiling, washing the ceiling in brightness. She grew frightened by the intensity of the light, hoping it wouldn't wake her father, but her fear was assuaged when the glow, as though reading her mind, gave out one quick burst of intense white light before shooting through the ceiling.

Mocha let out one quick bark, as though saying, "Wow!"

The room seemed to breathe and expand along with her breath and her father's breath, and even along with Mocha's breath. All one energy, breathing and expanding. Then slowly, darkness and stillness filled the room, gentle and peaceful. Even the grandfather clock seemed to tick more softly.

Mocha cocked his head to one side.

Zoe rubbed his ear. "Don't worry, Mocha. Everything's going to be okay."

She stepped out of the den and out the front door into the night. She looked up at the stars. The veil of city lights didn't obscure their true beauty as they twinkled naked before her. They seemed so close, close enough for her to reach out and pluck one, and she did. She held the star in the palm of her hand, closed her fingers over it and made a wish, a wish for her father.

She looked back up at the stars and saw how each one stood alone in its beauty, yet created a divine design with the others, and she wondered how anyone could live their entire life surrounded by city lights and not see the stars as she thought God intended for them to be seen. She drew in a deep breath, and the cold air stung her lungs. She turned to run back into the house, but something from the night sky caught her eye. She looked up. A golden glow shot across the heavens, leaving a long trail of sparkling citrine crystals. Night seemed to hold them for a moment before gently releasing them to gracefully fall and melt into the darkness.

Zoe smiled.

The heavens seemed to be smiling too.

***

The next morning, Zoe arose from bed and threw on her sweatpants and sweatshirt.

Nicole rolled over. "What are you doing up so early? It's not even seven o'clock."

"I have something to do."

"What could be more important than sleep?"

Without answering, Zoe left the bedroom, quietly shutting the door behind her. She went downstairs to the den. Her dad wasn't there.

"Good morning, Laurel," Zoe said, entering the kitchen.

"Good morning, Zoe," Laurel said, dumping flour into a mixer. "My goodness, you're up early."

Zoe eyed a bowl of blueberries on the counter. She popped one into her mouth. "Where's Dad?"

"He's in the greenhouse."

Zoe stepped outside. The early morning chill sent shivers through her body. She quickly followed the flagstone path through a garden that perhaps in the spring boasted of crocus and daffodils. She crossed over a small footbridge, then followed the dirt path leading to the greenhouse. She opened the door and stepped inside, into the warmth.

"Good morning, Zoe," her father said, looking up from a tomato plant.

"Good morning."

"Come look at this one," he said. "Isn't this tomato a beauty? Early Girl."

"It looks great, Dad."

"Oh, I forgot. You don't especially like tomatoes, do you?"

"Not especially."

"You might when you get older. Tastes change." He clipped off a leaf that had turned brown. "You're sure up early this morning."

"It's our last day together," she said. "I thought we could just hang out for a while."

Zoe glanced up at him, and she thought she detected a hint of sparkle in his blue eyes.

"Nicole up yet?" he asked.

"She's still sleeping. The only time she doesn't talk. Oh,

wait. She actually does talk in her sleep sometimes. I know. Hard to believe." Zoe laughed.

"It's good to hear you laugh," her dad said, picking a tomato from the vine and placing it into a wicker basket. "You haven't been doing enough of that since you've been here." He picked up a watering can. "Do you want to help me water some of these herbs?"

She nodded and grabbed a watering can. The smell of mint tickled her nose and she sneezed. She breathed in the scent of basil and thought of her mom's homemade spaghetti sauce.

"So," her dad said, "tell me again who this Dylan guy is."

She stopped watering and let out a heavy sigh.

"Zoe, I know Nicole has always been a talker," he said, putting the can down, "but I want to hear it from you."

"He's just a guy I like." She paused. "It's complicated."

"And that's the guy you were in the car accident with?"

She nodded. "He's not all bad," she said. "He loves poetry, especially Poe and Gibran."

"Well, he can't be all bad if he reads poetry, especially from the works of those two, although interestingly enough, quite the contrast." He leaned against the bench. "Zoe, is there anything else you'd like to tell me?"

Everything.

She wanted to tell him everything.

About how she'd died that day, gone to heaven, and talked with her grandma, and how she now heals the sick. Just like that. Simple. Easy. No big deal.

She wanted to tell him about the meetings she attended.

And all the other kids, kids just like her. And how liberating and empowering it was to be a part of a group that was so understanding and validating. And how they never abuse their power. Well, maybe just a wee bit, but only in dire circumstances and only after very careful consideration.

She wanted to tell him about how wise and intuitive Gabriel was, and how adorable and loveable Michael was. How wonderful they all were! But she couldn't. And in that moment, she felt sad.

She shook her head. "I'm good," she said.

He moved over to a tarragon plant. "I can't believe that in only a few more years you'll be off to college like Nicole," he said, pouring water over the dry soil.

Zoe felt a tinge of resentment and a slight jab to her heart. Why did everyone expect her to be like Nicole? She didn't want to be like her. Why couldn't anyone understand that? What would it take before she felt validated and appreciated by her family for who she was?

The greenhouse door creaked open and a breeze blew in. It felt refreshingly cool on her face and on the back of her neck. The fragrance of lavender filled the air and she breathed it in, deeply, relaxing into the moment.

"Dad, I don't want to be like Nicole," she said. "I want to be like me. I like me. Well, most of the time I like me. I do want to go on to school, but probably not college. Like a trade school to study art and design. Not medical stuff like Nicole, but artsy stuff like me."

"You were always good with that art stuff."

"I'll paint something for you when I get back. I'll send it to you."

"That'd be great." He sat down on a stool. "I want you to know that I'm surprised and humbled that you even wanted to spend more time with me. When you first got here, it was obvious you didn't want to, but I can't blame you."

"I'm glad I did come."

"So I'm not the big jerk after all."

"No, Dad, you're not a jerk. I'm sorry."

"You, my dear child, have nothing to be sorry for. I'm the one who should be sorry."

"Dad, really, it's—"

He held up his hand. "I owe you and Nicole an apology. Something I've never done. I've never said I'm sorry for not being a dad. And I am. I'm sorry."

He ran his hands through his thinning hair. "I can't believe how caught up I got in living my life without any regard for anyone else. There's nothing more important to me than you and Nicole, and I sure wish I would've realized that long before now. Long before this illness took hold."

She wanted to run to him, wrap her arms around him and hold him. But why she couldn't bring herself to do that either, she didn't know. And it didn't matter that she sensed her grandma's presence. She knew she wasn't ready to be as vulnerable before him as he was being with her, and all she could do was say, "There's still time."

He shook his head. "I wonder sometimes why it can take so long to figure things out, feel comfortable in our own skin. And by the time we do, it's often too late."

She took a step toward him. "Dad, it's not too late. That's what I'm trying to tell you."

A rumbling sounded across the sky, and droplets of rain plopped down on the polycarbonate roof, beaded up, and slithered down the sides like snakes.

He got up off his stool. Zoe thought he was going to give her a hug. She didn't know if she was ready for him to hug her, hold her. Another breeze blew in, a strong breeze that seemed to encourage her. She moved toward him and allowed him to wrap his arms around her. She hugged him back. They held each other for a few moments, and she wondered if he was tearing up too. As they stood in their embrace, lightning lit up the sky and thunder rolled. Zoe smiled in her tears. The heavens seemed to be applauding.

"Come on, kiddo," he said. "Let's get into the house before we get caught out here in the rain."

She linked one arm with her father's arm, and with the other, grabbed the basket full of tomatoes. Together they made their way back into the kitchen and to the sweet aroma of blueberry pancakes and maple syrup.

After breakfast, Nicole helped Laurel clean up, and Zoe packed their bags while their dad rested in the den.

Zoe carried the bags to the car with Mocha on her heels. She tossed the bags into the trunk. Mocha brushed his head against her leg.

"That thing with Dad, Mocha, it's our little secret," she said, kneeling down to rub his ears. "No one but you and I will ever know."

She ran back into the house. Mocha ran ahead of her. She peeked into the den. Her dad slept peacefully with Mocha now by his side, his tail wagging expectantly. She tiptoed over to her dad and kissed his pale cheek. His flesh felt cold. He lay motionless. Both he and the room seemed too quiet, too still, as though Death had sneaked in on tiptoe before her.

She poked him in the arm. Nothing. Again.

My god, I've killed him.

Then his nose twitched and he turned over and mumbled something.

The breath she had been holding escaped, and she laughed a nervous laugh. She pulled the blanket up around him and tucked him in, something he had never done for her. She took one last look at him. He seemed so peaceful in his dreams. She couldn't bring herself to speak the words, *I love you*, and she didn't know why.

"Ready?" Nicole asked, poking her head into the den.

"Ready," said Zoe.

The girls gave Laurel a hug good-bye and thanked her for everything.

"Travel well and enjoy the journey," Laurel said.

"We will," the girls said.

After one quick stop for gas, sodas, and a gift for Christopher, they headed out. Zoe suggested they take Highway 285, and when she saw the look of shock on her sister's face, she laughed.

"I want to take Laurel's advice," she said. "Enjoy the journey!"

"What's gotten into you? Wait," Nicole said, holding up her hand. "Don't answer that."

And Zoe and Nicole did enjoy the journey. Zoe relaxed

into the beauty of the towering ponderosa pines and aspens and thought about her dad. She felt she could now hold him close in her heart and that no one needed to know what she had done. At least for now, anyway. And that thing about the universe? Maybe Joanna was right. Maybe the Universe really was on her side.

Once Zoe and her sister arrived home, the questions seemed endless. How was the trip? How are Laurel and your dad? Are you hungry? And Christopher couldn't seem to get enough hugs and kisses from them. Zoe gladly obliged before handing Christopher his gift, as promised.

"A dinosaur!" said Christopher. "I love him." He hugged it close to his cheek. "Thank you, Zoe."

"You're welcome, Christopher," she said.

Zoe passed on the snack offered by Mom and ran upstairs to her bedroom. She plopped down on her bed and pulled her cell from her tote.

"You should tell me what to do more often," she said.

"Zoe?" Gabriel said.

"I want you to know that I'm glad I went."

"Sounds like everything worked out okay," he said.

"This forgiveness thing is hard," she said, "but I think I'm beginning to understand that there really isn't anything to forgive."

"We're all beautifully flawed," he said.

"We are," she said. "Beautifully."

She hit the End button.

She had one more call to make.

After all, she just had to brag to Dylan about those stars.

Twenty-Nine

"Zoe, can you give me a hand?" Adam asked.

Zoe put down the hooks and wire and hustled over to Adam. Together they stood the tri-fold art panel upright, unfolded it, and carefully locked it into place.

"Look familiar?" she asked, pointing to a brownish stain on the white fabric.

"That's exactly why I asked for your help," he said. "I don't want a repeat of what happened last year." He held up his finger and looked at the small scar. "It hurts all over again just thinking about it."

She grabbed his finger and gave it a quick kiss. "Better?"

"Much," he said, smiling. "Where were you last year when I needed that."

"Mad at you, remember?"

Adam thought about it for a moment. "I do remember now. You were mad at me because I just happened to mention that I thought Meagan was hot."

"You were practically about to do her right there in science lab."

He shook his head. "I still can't believe you got so mad."

Zoe paused and glanced down. "I wanted you to tell me that you thought I was hot."

Adam stood dumbfounded, confused. "I've always thought we had this silent understanding between us that no words could ever express," he said. "That we were friends, good friends, great friends, and nothing could ever change that. Not even a stupid guy fantasy about your long-lost friend." He paused. "I'm sorry for what I said and for what I didn't."

She stood silent for a few moments. "And I'm sorry I got so mad."

"Come on," he said. "Let's get the rest of these panels up and the artwork hung."

Zoe grabbed the hooks and wire, and after the artwork was hung, Adam took a walk around the auditorium.

"What are you doing?" she asked. "It looks great."

"Checking for good feng shui," he replied.

"You're joking, right?"

He held up the palms of his hands and made big, sweeping arches. "It's all about the energy, Zoe, the positive flow of energy." He dropped his hands. "Might help us win tonight."

She shook her head and smiled at him. She sometimes thought he was plain silly, but she liked that about him. She wasn't too sure about that feng shui stuff, but either way, she hoped he was right about the flow of energy helping them win. She did feel confident about the two pieces she had entered; her watercolor landscape of aspens and snow-capped mountains, and her pencil drawing of her warrior princess standing proudly on a hilltop overlooking the city she was about to conquer from the enemy.

As she walked to her locker, she thought about that word, *enemy*, and wondered how there could be such a thing. If we're all swimming around in the same energy, breathing the same air, feeling the same heat of the sun on our bodies, looking toward the heavens at the same stars, galaxies and constellations that belonged to no one, yet everyone, how can there be enemies?

The words of Henry Wadsworth Longfellow echoed to her: "If we could read the secret history of our enemies, we should find in each man's life sorrow and suffering enough to disarm all hostility."

Wishful thinking on disarming all hostility, perhaps, and maybe wishful thinking on winning tonight, but if she did win, her art would be displayed right inside the main entrance of the high school along with the previous winners. She thought it only fair that students' art be held in equal esteem with the sports trophies. And if she didn't win, she would donate her work to the hospital's art program, where the cancer patients could look upon what Florence Nightingale might call "beautiful objects."

The clicking of heels on tile brought her out of her reverie.

"Zoe."

"Meagan?"

Zoe turned around and looked into the eyes of her long-lost friend and wondered when the punch line was coming.

But Meagan just stood there waiting, and Zoe wondered what she was waiting for. For her to throw her arms around her, hug her, and tell her how she'd missed her as her friend, her absolute best friend ever, because no one could ever take her place, and thank god she'd come to her senses and realized that we're all in this together, no one better than the other, and that the status thing is one big illusion, one big joke of the universe, and sadly, she'd fallen for it, poor thing. Oh, she's so glad they've mended their broken friendship, and let's pretend no one's feelings were hurt and that none of it mattered. None of it. It's all okay.

"Meagan, if you're after a story for the school paper, I'm not interested. Besides, if your entourage sees you talking to me, it could seriously take you down a few notches in the social stratosphere, or did you so honorably reinstate Vanessa as top Gospel Girl? I mean, the word is out. She never was crazy."

Meagan bit her lip. "I don't care about them right now, and I'm not here for a story. I wanted you to know that I'm sorry. I wanted you to know that my life was a hell of a lot more fun when you and Hailey were in it." Meagan paused. "I'm wondering if we could ever be friends again."

Zoe wondered if Meagan realized that she had lost more than her friendship, and if she had any idea of how much it hurts to be deserted by a friend for a status fix.

A different kind of drug.

Zoe took a long, hard look at her. "You mean now that I'm supposedly some big celebrity? I don't think so, Meagan. It doesn't work that way. I'll accept your apology, and spare you any further embarrassment. Your entourage is coming."

And with that, Zoe turned and headed toward the exit, feeling a little sad that life couldn't be the way it once was, but at the same time, feeling glad it wasn't. She realized that the letting go of old friends and old hurts wasn't always so easy, but when she did find herself letting go, it actually felt pretty damn good.

***

Zoe slipped into a black sundress she had snagged from her sister's closet. She wrapped a mint-green cashmere sweater, borrowed from her mom, around her shoulders. She strapped on her black sandals with three-inch heels and wondered if perhaps she shouldn't have practiced a few steps in them before tonight.

She stood in front of her mirrored closet doors and applied black mascara and light-coral lip gloss. She looked at her reflection and tossed her head, sending her strawberry curls dancing around her face. She grinned. She looked good, and she knew it.

Right at seven o'clock, the doors to the school auditorium opened wide and the crowd filtered in. Punch was being poured, refreshments were being served. Zoe poured Christopher a glass, while her parents helped themselves to refreshments. She wished her sister could have come, but Nicole had assured her that they'd celebrate after her win.

Zoe pointed in the direction of where her two art pieces were hung and told them to also check out Adam's art, which hung on the same panel as hers. She'd join them shortly. They meandered off, Christopher holding his dad's hand.

Dylan should be arriving any minute now.

She hadn't told her mom or Charles that she had invited him. They still weren't okay with him, but Zoe took the advice of Matt: "If you think that's what you want, go for it. Don't let anyone tell you how love is supposed to show up in your life."

She sometimes wondered about Matt and how he was doing and if he and his girlfriend ever got back together again. Maybe she'd see him again someday. Maybe she'd see his girlfriend come into the shop again. Perhaps to buy celebratory flowers. If she did, she would be sure to give her the best customer service ever.

She looked around the room, then glanced once again toward the entrance. At least Dylan had sounded excited about coming. She wished Hailey and Isabelle had shown the same enthusiasm, but when she had mentioned the art show to them in school, Hailey said something about track and Isabelle said something about music. Zoe wished now that she had been more supportive of their interests and talents.

She poured herself a glass of punch and thought back to the days before Hailey and Isabelle had labeled her as "too smart." The three of them would steal vodka from their parents' liquor cabinets, sneak it into school parties, pour themselves a glass of punch, slip into the girls' bathroom, pour in the magic, and drink away. It had been fun at the time.

She anxiously tapped her fingers on the refreshment table and realized that not only were her two best friends not coming, but it looked like Dylan wasn't coming either. She decided it didn't matter, that it had to not matter. She also realized that she probably looked pathetic standing there by herself with only refreshments and punch to keep her company. Just as she was about to head into the crowd to find her family, familiar voices called out her name.

Hailey? Isabelle? She slowly turned around. The three of them stood there for a moment, staring at one another. Zoe couldn't believe it. Her friends had actually come, and now that they were here, a feeling of discomfort swept over her, a feeling that took her by surprise.

Isabelle took a step forward. "We've missed you."

"We're sorry, Zoe," said Hailey. "Sorry we were kind of mean to you."

"Kind of?" said Zoe. "That was brutal. Pushing me aside like a—"

"A smart kid," Isabelle said, with a grin.

"Yeah, that," Zoe said.

"Forgive us?" Hailey asked.

Forgiveness. Why does it always seem so easy to do until one is actually asked to do it?

Zoe contemplated both questions for a few moments. She looked at them, not sure how to answer. She knew that she did miss them. She thought back to when Gabriel had talked about the ego, and how it can interfere with happiness. This is one moment in her life where happiness needed to rule, and in that realization, she nodded. The girls squealed and hugged one another. Hailey took Zoe's glass from her, refilled it, and filled one for herself and Isabelle.

"A toast," Hailey said. "A toast to the three of us. Friends forever."

"Friends forever," the three of them chimed as they raised their glasses. They tapped their plastic glasses together and downed their punch, and Zoe was glad it really was just punch.

"I'm glad you guys made it," Zoe said.

"We wouldn't miss you winning first place for anything," Isabelle said.

"And we haven't even seen your piece yet," Hailey said. "But we know when we're with a winner."

"Pieces," Zoe said. "Come on. I'll show them to you."

As they walked toward the panel, Zoe asked, "You guys didn't happen to see Dylan when you walked in, did you?"

"You two are back together?" Hailey asked.

Zoe smiled. "I guess the three of us do have a lot of catching up to do."

Isabelle put her arm around Zoe's shoulder. "I'll say, and we still want to hear about that voodoo that you do."

Zoe laughed. "Voodoo to you, maybe."

"We heard all about it on the news," Hailey said.

"You're a damn celebrity now," Isabelle said.

Zoe shrugged Isabelle's arm from her shoulder. "Please don't call me that, and please don't tell me that's why you're here."

"Zoe, I swear to you," Isabelle said." We've missed you. Not because of anything you've become, but because—"

"Because life totally sucks without you!" Hailey said, giving Zoe a punch in the arm.

The girls laughed and embraced.

"You guys rock," Zoe said.

The girls walked through the maze of panels. Zoe pointed to the panel that held hers.

"Up front and close to the judges," Isabelle said.

"I don't think being close to the judges' table means anything," Zoe said, grinning. "Even though I did place them there." And she burst out laughing, and Hailey and Isabelle laughed with her.

The girls walked back to the refreshment table and poured themselves another glass of punch. They munched on chips and crackers while chatting and laughing about how lame some of the pieces were and how could they have possibly made it into the show. "Were you bribed, Zoe, to hang some of those pieces?" "Okay, that's cruel." "Those will probably be the ones that win. It is subjective. Beauty is in the eye of the beholder." "Then they must be blind." And on and on they went, laughing and giggling as though nothing had ever come between them.

The sound of someone tapping the microphone interrupted their laughter. They turned and looked toward the stage.

"If I could have your attention, please," Mr. Martinez said. "If you would please finish your viewing of all this wonderful student art we have displayed here this evening, grab some punch and snacks if you like, then take a seat. We'll be starting the program in a few minutes, and shortly thereafter, the judges will announce the top five winners."

"Hey," Hailey said, pointing toward the entrance, "look who just showed up."

Zoe turned. Dylan stood in the doorway dressed in indigo jeans and black T-shirt. He held a sports bottle in one hand and the program in the other.

Isabelle turned to Zoe. "Damn, he's hot."

Zoe smiled and shook her head.

"Does he have a brother? Maybe even a cousin?" Isabelle asked before Hailey grabbed her arm.

"Isabelle and I will find some seats up front," Hailey said, practically dragging Isabelle with her. "See you in a bit."

Now they were all here. This was going to be the best night of her life. She could feel it.

Zoe zigzagged through the crowd, and when she finally reached Dylan, he leaned over and gave her a hug and a kiss on the lips. The hug was squishy, and the kiss was hard.

"Hmmm, fruity. I like it," he said, leaning in for another kiss. Zoe turned her face, and he planted a firm one on her cheek. His face felt sweaty, and his breath smelled like alcohol.

He stepped back and looked at her from head to toe, then let out a low whistle. "Looking hot, Zoe."

"Thank you," she said, looking into his dark eyes as though they were about to reveal an ugly truth about him, a truth she wasn't so certain she could handle right now.

He looked out over the crowd. "So, is there a big party after all this is over, because I'm ready to party," he said loudly, waving his sports bottle.

"No, Dylan, there's no party," she said.

He'd been drinking. But how much? She wasn't sure she wanted to know.

"Do you want to see my artwork?" she asked.

"Hell yeah."

Hell yeah? What was that? He's never sounded like that before.

She wasn't too sure she wanted to take him to see her art, but that's why he was here. To offer his support. She took his hand in hers and led him down the center aisle toward the panel. He stopped at one of the panels and leaned in close to look at an oil painting of a parrot.

"This is some real cool shit," he said.

Her eyes widened. Maybe she should forget this whole thing and show him to the door. But they were almost to the panel, her panel, with her art. Just a few more steps. And then, he did it. She quickly jumped back, but not before the smelly mess splattered all over her black sandals.

All eyes were on them now. Shock, disbelief, sadness, anger. She felt it all rush up inside. The warrior screaming. She looked at Hailey and Isabelle, their mouths agape, their eyes wide. Zoe turned and ran out of the auditorium, down the hall, and into the restroom. She leaned against the vanity, breathing deeply. Tears formed, then moistened her cheeks.

The restroom door slowly creaked open.

"Zoe, can we come in?" Hailey asked.

She nodded.

"We're sorry," Hailey said, stepping inside. "We know how much it meant for you to have him here."

"Security is escorting him out, and the janitor is cleaning it up," Isabelle said.

"It was going to be so perfect," Zoe said.

"We know."

"I was so looking forward to this night."

"We know."

"I'm such an idiot for thinking—"

"You're not an idiot," Hailey said, standing beside her.

"Here," said Isabelle, handing Zoe a tissue. "Your mascara is running."

Zoe wiped her eyes, then slipped off her sandals.

"I'll rinse them off for you," said Isabelle.

Zoe wiped her feet, slipped her sandals back on, reapplied her mascara and lip gloss, smoothed down her curls, and straightened her dress.

"Looking way hot again," Hailey said.

Zoe turned to Hailey and Isabelle. "You're the best friends ever." She hugged them both. "I'm ready."

The girls took their seats close to the stage. The countdown began, and with each name called, Zoe grew even more nervous. Mr. Martinez named the fifth winner, the fourth winner, the third winner, and life seemed to move in slow motion. Zoe took a deep breath. Her name would soon be announced. She could feel it.

"Second place goes to . . . Adam Pelanowski!"

Zoe practically jumped out of her seat in enthusiastic joy for Adam. His eyes met hers as he walked past, and she waved and smiled at him. He smiled back and winked as if to say, *You're next.*

A silence hung over the audience now. The final name. The grand prize. Funny, Zoe didn't even know what the grand prize was. Didn't matter.

"And the first place winner is . . ."

A pause. A hush.

"Rebecca Cunningham!"

And the name seemed to echo throughout the auditorium.

And echo and echo and echo.

Zoe gasped. *Who the hell is Rebecca Cunningham?*

Isabelle, Hailey, and Zoe turned and watched as a freckle-faced, red-haired, lanky girl made her way down the center aisle to the stage.

Zoe recognized her as that quiet girl. The one who always sat in the back of art class and never said anything. Never shared anything. Never went to parties, dances, events. A nothing. A nobody. A quiet, nothing, nobody. Quiet, nothing nobodies don't win. Don't ever win. Do they?

Mr. Martinez held up her artwork.

Zoe was dumbfounded. *That? That won? It's a stupid bird. A stupid parrot. Okay, so he's a green-winged macaw perched on a branch in a lush emerald rain forest with what looks like dew on leaves and sunlight filtering through mist. Animal and forest scenes must be so in now.* But the more she gazed upon the painting, the more she realized that it might not be so stupid after all. It had a balance of great color and texture, the light was perfect, and the expression on the parrot was intriguing. An expression of absolute contentment.

She slumped in her chair, then clapped only because everyone else did. The tapping of the microphone brought her out of her pity party. It was one of the judges tapping, and she wondered why the judge felt it necessary to tap that thing. It was irritating, and now even more so.

"We have another announcement before we end this evening," the judge said. "But afterward, mingle, get to know one another. There's more punch and food. And now, I'd like to hand the microphone back over to Mr. Martinez."

Light clapping again.

Zoe yawned.

"Congratulations to all of our winners, and thank you to all who participated, and for the parents who are here showing support for our youth," Mr. Martinez said, holding up his hand to silence the applause.

The room grew quiet.

"I'd like to take this moment to say a few words. A few words about a very special young lady, a lady who epitomizes what it means to mature as an artist, who exemplifies what it means to rise above adversity. Her resilience and spirit and courage have inspired us all, to not only be better artists, but better people, and we . . . "

Zoe turned to Hailey and Isabelle and whispered, "Who died?"

Hailey and Isabelle fought back giggles, and Zoe covered her mouth to stifle her own laugher.

" . . . and so this evening, we are here not only to honor the artwork of our very talented students, but also to honor a very special person for her creative spirit and for the unselfish acts of gentleness and kindness she bestows upon the sick . . . "

Zoe suddenly grew nervous. She shifted in her seat. Haley and Isabelle looked at her. She shrugged. And wondered.

" . . . and her knowledge and love of art she so graciously and generously shares with the patients at St. Francis

Hospital. And so, without further ado, the First Annual Creative Spirit Award goes to . . . Zoe Weber."

Zoe clasped her hands to her mouth.

Hailey and Isabelle let out a yelp and hugged her tightly. The auditorium erupted in clapping, loud and enthusiastic clapping. Zoe stood up, and suddenly felt shy, humbled, grateful, and somewhat awkward. Isabelle gave her a slight nudge toward the stage, and as Zoe headed in that direction, people reached out to shake her hand, to pat her on the back, to say "congratulations," "good job," "we're so proud of you."

Ascending the stairs, she felt as though she was floating in her three-inch heels. She walked across the stage, still with that floaty feeling. Mr. Martinez handed her the First Annual Creative Spirit Award. Zoe took the award in her hands, feeling the warmth of the amethyst crystal base. She looked at the figurine perched atop. A hummingbird in flight, delighting in the nectar of a pink flower. Its body emerald green and wings iridescent purple, all of it arrayed in tiny citrine crystals. It was beautiful, perhaps even more beautiful than anything she had ever seen, even the gifts in her mom's shop.

She grinned and smiled and blinked back tears as she looked out over the audience. They were all standing now, clapping and cheering. She spotted Christopher sitting atop his dad's shoulders, waving and clapping. She waved back. Charles clapped and smiled proudly, as did her mom, who gave Charles a quick peck on the cheek.

And before she knew it, the tears fell. She decided she didn't care, because after all, what's a tear or two?

Thirty

After school the next day, Zoe and the other art students headed to the auditorium to take down the displays and store away the panels until the next show. Zoe slid her art into her portfolio. She needed to get to the hospital to donate her artwork before Maggie left, but as she was about to head out of the auditorium, she heard an unfamiliar voice asking her to wait up.

She turned around.

It was the freckled-faced, lanky girl.

"Hi, Zoe," Rebecca said.

"Hi, Rebecca." Zoe looked at her, feeling bad now that she never congratulated her on her first-place win.

A small group of art students, including Adam, had gathered around Rebecca, each one holding their work.

"We had a little meeting," Rebecca said.

"A meeting?" Zoe asked.

Rebecca continued, "We decided that we don't want our artwork displayed next to the sports trophies and awards. We decided that we'd like to go with you to the hospital."

Adam stepped forward. "We'd rather have our work displayed in the patient rooms, where we think it will do the most good."

"And where it will be the most appreciated," another boy said.

"Unlike here at the school," a girl said, "where most of the students couldn't care less."

"Yeah!" they all said.

Zoe stood in front of them, shocked. Her voice betrayed her as she tried to speak. She felt a tugging at her heart, a lump in her throat. What does one say to such kind words? When she finally did find her voice, it seemed so inadequate when all she could muster up was a simple "thank you."

"So, what are we waiting for?" Adam said, thrusting his fist into the air. "To the hospital."

"To the hospital!" they said, punching their fists into the air. "To the hospital!"

***

Maggie stood in her office as student after student came in to donate their artwork. Some of the art was placed on her desk, some on the chairs, some against the wall, some on the floor. Each student retreated back into the corridor, until the last of the students had donated theirs, and before Maggie knew it, her office was overflowing with beautiful objects.

"Thank you all so very much," Maggie said. "You have no idea how much your thoughtful generosity will be appreciated."

After the students left, Maggie thanked Zoe for not only the donation, but also for having the courage to stand on the hospital steps and reveal her gift, and by doing so, restore her reputation.

"It is a little freaky," Zoe said, "this gift and all, but I do like to think that somewhere, somehow, Grandma is smiling."

"I'm sure she is, Zoe, I'm sure she is." She looked around at the art pieces. "I hope you'll come back and help me hang these. And, continue to help with the art program."

"Aunt Maggie?"

"Yes?"

"At what point did you know about my gift?"

Maggie smiled. "Does it matter?"

Zoe grinned and shook her head. She gave her aunt a quick hug.

As she walked to her car, she wondered why the thought of continuing to help in the art program left her feeling anxious, the same feeling she had when she was going to visit her dad. But that had turned out okay, so maybe going back to the hospital would be okay too.

She climbed into her car and was about to drive to the shop when her cell phone rang. It was her dad. He thanked her for the letter and for the painting of the two of them standing on a cliff overlooking a lavender field. And she thought that he sounded good. Really good. He told her that he was feeling much better, but that he wasn't out of the woods yet. He told her that his recovery would be long and hard, but he felt as though he was finally gaining ground.

He thanked her for being unselfish in her desire to help him. He admitted that he was shocked to read in her letter of her gift of healing, and he told her that he felt blessed to have such a wonderful daughter, something he knew all along.

He told her that, no, he hadn't said anything to Laurel. What she had done, per her wishes, would stay between the two of them.

Warmth passed through her and she felt her nose growing moist. When she told him good-bye, she hoped he hadn't noticed the crack in her voice.

Forgiveness.

It was beginning to feel good.

She decided she had one very important call to make before she drove to the shop. She stared at her cell phone, took a deep breath, then punched in the number.

Dylan answered.

She told him it was over.

Very diplomatic. Very mature. Very easy. Much easier than she had thought it would be. She told him that she wished him well. "So, good-bye, Dylan," she said. No spite. No anger. Just good-bye.

He didn't seem to get it. Had he had been drinking again? His response? "Okay, see you around sometime."

Sure you will.

And now, for that one last thing.

She walked into Lacey's Herb and Flower Shoppe, grabbed a bundle of English lavender and a bundle of baby's breath, and tied it all together with a purple gossamer ribbon. She told her mom she had something to do.

The wind at the top of the hill was gusty and felt cool on her face. She held her arms over the flowers, protecting them from the wind. She looked out over the town. From here, she could see it all: St. Francis Hospital, the historic district, her high school, the ice arena where she and Dylan had had their first kiss, and the creek where they'd had their last. Why did the town seem so different now, as though she was seeing it for the very first time?

She turned her attention back to the cemetery, looking for that familiar landmark. She spotted it and walked toward the two towering blue spruce trees. She stood between them and paced off the sixty or so steps. Then she saw it, the gray granite stone that read "Lacey Elizabeth Ellis." She knelt down and placed the lavender bouquet against the stone.

She sat cross-legged and tugged at the grass. She wasn't so sure where to begin, and she hoped that her words would not create strange looks from the others who had come to pay their respects to their loved ones. But then, she was starting to get used to the strange looks and the whispers. *Isn't that her? That girl from the news? That girl from the hospital? You know, back in the day, they would have . . . Her grandmother was a . . .*

Zoe tried to block it all out, but it wasn't always easy. She figured not much in her life would be easy anymore. She thought about how much her life had changed since the accident, which for lack of a better word was what she called it, because why bother? Why bother telling anyone that she'd come to realize that it wasn't an accident at all, but something that needed to happen. She now believed that the universe was not a chaotic place—it's all sacred, a divine design—and that sometimes life just had to be a mystery, however confusing at times, with little sparks of magic glittering along the path making it all worthwhile.

And, what to say to her grandma? The thoughts and words kept tripping around her head and tongue. No words seemed adequate. She knew in her heart how she felt, but how does one articulate such deep feelings? The words don't exist in our limited language, and was there any language even capable of conveying such sentiments?

So, she spoke no words, knowing that it wasn't necessary because somehow, somewhere, Grandma Lacey was listening and understanding her every unspoken word. She relaxed into that knowing.

And then, a movement, a fluttering.

She looked closely. A fairy?

The fairy winked at Zoe, her purple wings rapidly beating. The fairy hovered over the lavender, then waved her wand, surrounding Zoe in the sweet, delicious scent. Then, with one large sweep, she waved the scent high into the air and on into the heavens.